JOURNEY'S CALL

JOURNEY RUSSO SERIES: BOOK ONE

MARY STONE

AMY WILSON

❀ Created with Vellum

This book is dedicated to the loyal readers who have journeyed with me thus far. Your steadfast support and enthusiasm have been my inspiration. Thank you for believing in my stories and for being an integral part of this exciting new chapter.

DESCRIPTION

When fate calls, death could be dialing.

Journey Russo is no stranger to the harsh shadows cast by secrets. The fire that claimed her family when she was just thirteen years old left her life scorched by mystery and loss. Raised by her grandparents amidst the embers of her past, Journey transformed her trauma into resolve, forging a path as an FBI special agent. But beneath her determined facade lies a lingering fear of fire and the unhealed scars of betrayal.

In a world of hidden flames, truth is her only weapon.

As she steps onto the crime scene at Pittsburg gun store, Journey confronts not just a perplexing case, but the echoes of a past that refuse to be silenced. The victims, from different walks of life, share disturbingly similar fatal wounds—a bullet to the stomach and a brutal head injury. With only a dead body, missing guns, and no clear suspects, Journey is propelled into a mystery that tests her skills.

Though she loves nothing more than solving a good puzzle, the investigation takes a startling twist when she discovers a link between the case and a brutal cult that haunts her dreams. And as more victims emerge, Journey's past and present collide, forcing her to confront the demons she thought she'd left behind.

Before the body count rises.

Journey's Call is book one of the adrenaline-charged new Journey Russo series by bestselling author Mary Stone, where secrets have lethal consequences, and the pursuit of truth is as dangerous as the secrets themselves.

1

On Sundays, Sam Faulkner had a ritual. And much to his Catholic mother's chagrin, that didn't involve attending mass.

Sam wasn't a religious man. To him, Sundays were a day for silent reflection...on the week's sales numbers. He'd close Faulkner's Guns & Ammo by four, send everyone home, lock the doors, and settle in for an evening of bookkeeping. A tumbler of bourbon in his hand, the tempting scent of *souvlaki* wafting in the air from the Greek restaurant two doors down, and stacks of paperwork spread across the counter.

April fourth.

Sam double-checked the date his employee had listed on the background check for a customer looking to buy a Sig Sauer P365. He didn't have to review his team's PICS requests—the Pennsylvania Instant Check System was online, and most mistakes errored out quickly.

He did it anyway.

Sam reviewed every piece of documentation going in and

out of his shop. Selling firearms was serious business, and he sure as hell wouldn't let a clerical error cost him his shop.

With a wife and two daughters to consider in a tanking economy, he knew his family wouldn't survive on Tammie's salary alone. Sam had college funds to consider for his girls to receive all the opportunities they needed for their futures.

His business couldn't just follow the rules, couldn't just cover monthly expenses—it had to thrive.

Faulkner's Guns & Ammo was dead quiet. Sam groaned as he lifted his head, his neck sore from hours spent hunched over the showroom counter. The office would've been a more logical place to work, but the air conditioning didn't reach back there, and the tiny desk left little room to spread out.

Anyway, the shop was empty, and he had all evening. Tammie and the girls knew not to expect him home before midnight on Sundays. He'd make up the lost time with them during the summer. Take the family on a vacation while the girls had their break from school.

Glancing around the showroom, Sam smiled with pride. Unlike his competitors, who stuffed their shops like they were planning for Armageddon, Sam avoided clutter, which he believed led to better sales. Black steel against white walls. Give buyers too many choices, and analysis paralysis sent them back out the door with their money still in their pockets.

And with his setup, he could see customers from every angle, no matter where they stood.

Sam had just finished reviewing the distributor invoices when the lights went out.

He counted to ten. The backup generator normally didn't take long to kick in. He'd installed it to make sure his alarm system remained functional. Couldn't be too careful. But when he got to twelve, the darkness lingered.

Tiny hairs on the back of Sam's neck tingled. The generator should've kicked in. He'd tested the system last week.

Any second now.

The generator remained silent.

He was just pushing to his feet when a crash reverberated up the hallway like a thunderclap. It sounded like a box of ammo cans tipped over in the stockroom, but that wasn't possible. Not by itself.

Ominous silence followed.

Someone was in the store.

Sam's brain raced as he stood still. Moments like this were the reason he'd designed the place the way he had. Cameras in every corner. A generator for backup power. Even a silent alarm that rang straight to security dispatch. But nothing was working, none of the interior emergency lights coming up. There wasn't any reason for his backup system to fail.

Unless someone knew about it.

That realization hit Sam like a punch. Was he under siege by one of his own, an employee who knew his security system?

His fingers grasped for the comforting solid steel of his Glock, Ole Bastard.

Game on, rat.

He took a steadying breath and considered his next move.

If this was a burglary, the rat would most likely stay in the stockroom. A team member, if this was an inside job, would know the snatch-and-grab was easier there. Items on the sales floor were bolted and tethered to prevent theft.

Sam stealthed toward the short hallway leading to the break room, stockroom, and office. Slowing his breath, he listened for the intruder. His knuckles whitened as his grip tightened on Ole Bastard.

Whoever you are, you picked the wrong place to rob.

They had to be close. The hallway wasn't that wide or long.

The whispered squeal of rubber against concrete sent Sam's heart hammering against his ribs. A sudden burst of air rushed past.

Sam cursed under his breath. The intruder had just made a mad dash for the showroom, and he hadn't reacted quick enough to get a shot off.

A fast-moving shadow sped by the shop's window, briefly illuminated against the parking lot lights. He couldn't make out any detail, male or female, armed or not. It was too dark.

The rat surfaced again near the shop entrance. Maybe they'd changed their mind, decided to flee. Or maybe they were assessing the space.

Go ahead. Case the joint. You'll never know it better than I do.

Sam crept back to the front display cases where he'd been working. The wall display would provide cover from behind, and maybe, with the outside light coming in through the windows, he could spot the rat.

Gun at the ready, Sam crouched behind the glass display counter and scanned the showroom.

A deeper darkness fell over him as the rat dove across the counter. Sam fired blindly at the shadow.

A second shot followed the first, but not from Sam's gun.

Flames tore through Sam's gut as the force of the impact threw him against the display. He slid down to the floor.

Fire spread everywhere now, digging into his belly, racing down his legs. Even his ears screamed with it, a tornado of searing pain threatening to explode his skull. Death stood like a towering black mass at his feet, ready to sweep him away into the abyss.

Sam tried to kick, but Death only laughed and brought a heavy heel down on his leg.

"You won't be needing this anymore." Death leaned close, toeing Ole Bastard from his limp hand. Tequila on his breath. "*Tsk. Tsk.* Who'd expect a gun store owner to be such a bad shot?"

That voice. Where had Sam heard it before?

"This is the end for you. But you know that already, don't you?"

Sam wasn't dead yet. The wound was serious, but it hadn't killed him. He reached for his pistol, stretching his fingers. Forgetting he'd been disarmed.

"Guns, guns everywhere." Death grabbed him by the jaw, twisting his face to look at the display directly overhead. "And not one of them can save you."

The edges of Sam's vision darkened, the thought of sinking into unconsciousness bringing a sense of peace. But he couldn't rest yet. If he just made it to the counter, maybe he could trigger the silent alarm.

Had he already? Maybe he was doing it now?

The black abyss pressed heavily on his body.

Sam's mind found refuge, slipping into the pond near his house. The one from his childhood. The water his memory conjured cooled the fire scorching his body and whispered a promise to end his pain.

It tempted him to sink further into the darkness. Sam blinked against the seduction.

As his eyes struggled open, he focused on the figure towering over him. Death gripped an object, a little bigger than his palm. He weighed it in his hands.

Sam's eyes closed again, blocking out the looming figure as he prayed to get back to the image of the pond near his house.

Maybe his wife and kids could join him this time.

"This'll work." The voice ripped through Sam's head, shredding his peaceful drift into oblivion. "It's perfect."

Sam recognized the voice. His eyes shot open again.

It was an accident...

Thunder clapped against Sam's head, and lightning whipped through his vision. For a moment he saw Death's face, but the white-hot pain that followed stole the memory and replaced it with rippling echoes of agony. He screamed and kicked, as if that might somehow make the pain stop.

"It'll be over soon."

Sam closed his eyes and allowed the darkness to take his pain away.

2

Special Agent Journey Russo was experiencing a rare Sunday with nothing to do.

Boredom was unsettling. Journey had to keep herself busy, so she'd taken to the kitchen in her apartment, along with her sister. It was quite the complex dance in the smallish space, with her playing baker and Michelle in the role of chef.

"You know you want one of these banana chocolate chip muffins." Journey waved the platter beneath Michelle's nose.

"Not now." Her sister pushed the dessert out of the way and reached for a spoon from the utensil jar beside the stove. "I haven't finished cooking the chicken yet."

This was how food prep went with Journey and her adopted sister, Michelle Timmer. Michelle cooked some amazing dishes based on instincts and vibes. Journey followed a baking recipe to the letter to reproduce some grandma's sought-after gravestone recipe. Despite their siblinghood, they were different in many, many ways.

To Journey, she couldn't have looked more different from her sister. She always felt like a giant next to Michelle's petite frame, even though they differed by a mere four inches. Her eyes were a dark indigo compared to Michelle's liquid blue. And though at one point they'd both had brownish hair, Journey still sported her natural color, but Michelle's was currently dyed an inky black.

Despite the night-and-day differences in their appearance, they were sisters in every way that truly mattered, raised by Journey's grandparents when they were teens. Though not related by blood, Journey and Michelle were as close as twins. They needed each other as much as any two people could.

Michelle turned her attention away from the stove to Journey. "Why are you anxiety-baking anyway? It's your day off."

Journey pulled off a small chunk of muffin and popped it into her mouth. "I'm not anxious. I just don't know what to do with so much free time."

Michelle wagged the spoon at her. "Ooh, a whole twenty-four hours to yourself. How will you possibly survive?"

"Why do you think I invited you over to make your tasty chicken piccata?"

"Because I'm your only friend. Or, more likely, because if it weren't for these dinners, we'd never see each other, even though we only live three blocks apart."

Journey smiled, then turned away as tears burned her eyes. She'd come so close to losing Michelle two years ago.

"Fair point. We don't hang out as often as we should." Which was pretty bad, considering they worked out of the same FBI Pittsburgh field office. They'd each been there two years now, Journey as a special agent in Violent Crimes and Michelle in Crime Scene Investigation. They loved their jobs, not exactly beating allegations of workaholism.

A few years earlier, Michelle would've happily accepted

that title. But she'd gained a better sense of work-life balance since...

Journey shook her head. She didn't want to think about why Michelle needed balance in the first place. Or why she'd left her job in Chicago and moved to Pennsylvania.

As for Journey, she was due for an intervention, as long as she could schedule it between cases.

"I'm here now. Catch me up on all your news." Michelle leaned over the skillet, breathing in the fragrance of the sauce and smiling at her creation.

The muffins weren't holding Journey's hunger at bay. Not with garlic, butter, and lemon teasing her nose. She busied herself by pulling two plates from the cupboard. "Did I tell you about my new case partner?"

"A little." Michelle stirred the bubbling sauce. "Lucas, something?"

"Sullivan. Technically, it's Lucas, but he gives you a death stare if you call him that. Just transferred into Violent Crimes from White Collar."

"Would I recognize him?"

Journey considered. While the Pittsburgh field office wasn't the largest in the country, it employed dozens of agents dedicated to serving twenty-five counties in Pennsylvania and all of West Virginia. It would be easy not to know everyone in the four-story building.

"Seen anyone who looks like James Dean dressed in a *Men in Black* costume?"

Michelle grinned. "Sounds like I'm missing out."

"Anyway, I think he'll make an excellent partner." Journey set down the plates and turned toward the silverware drawer. "He brought me coffee several times last week without asking."

"Iced, creamy, and with seventeen sugars." Every time

Michelle joked about Journey's coffee preferences, she added one packet of sugar to the list.

"Yum." Journey took her coffee only one way—black, extra hot. Perfect. "You know that's just the way I like it. Didn't have to tell him twice either."

"So competent. As if black, extra hot is difficult to remember."

"Whatever it takes to get good coffee. Anyway, he doesn't talk about his personal life much, but I know one delicious tidbit." She bumped the silverware drawer closed with her hip and waited for Michelle to take the bait.

Michelle, however, remained focused on thickening her butter sauce.

Journey didn't have the patience to wait. "His daughter's name is Hallie."

Michelle didn't respond verbally, but the way her sauce stirring went from passive to aggressive confirmed she'd heard her.

"You remember Hallie?" Journey struggled to hold her expression neutral. "As in Hallie with the hollyhock hair?"

"I'm ignoring you."

No, you're not.

In tenth-grade English, Michelle had been out sick with the flu when the teacher gave the class an assignment to write a modern fairy tale about an everyday problem. Michelle had written a story about talking tortoises and a girl named Hallie with flowers for hair.

Being absent, Michelle had missed the examples of modern fairy tales they read in class, so she didn't understand what a *modern* fairy tale included.

"What was my favorite line?" Laughing, Journey pretended to think, but in reality, she knew she could recite the entire tale for the rest of her life. "Oh, right. 'But, Mr.

Tortoise, you have a short, little neck and a tiny, bitty nose, and couldn't possibly sniff my strands of violets and rose.'"

"Still ignoring you."

"I wonder if hollyhocks grow well in patio planters." Hand pressed to her belly, Journey moved to the sliding glass door and looked out onto her balcony. "It's April fourth. Spring is just around the corner."

"I'm ignoring you. Haven't you heard?"

All evidence to the contrary.

Still...the chicken piccata was ready. If Journey didn't quit teasing, Michelle wasn't going to share.

"Fine." She heaved an overly dramatic sigh. "I thought you'd be ready to laugh about it after all these years, but I guess some people just can't move on from the past."

"You're the one living in the past here, so I wouldn't know."

They sat together at the sturdy, vintage farm table Journey had picked up from an antique shop. The refurnished solid-fir surface was scratched, but Journey loved the character it added, so she hadn't sanded out the nicks.

While Michelle passed the salad, Journey poured iced tea.

"In another small-world coincidence, I've actually crossed paths with Lucas before." Journey tore a chunk of bread from a warmed baguette and handed the basket to her sister. "He was on the WC team handling the investigation into The Chosen nearly ten years ago."

The Chosen.

Journey shook her head, mentally rewinding to the cult's strange beginnings.

Against the tumultuous backdrop of 1969, amid the Vietnam War and the Civil Rights Movement, two returning soldiers, the Leopold brothers, found themselves disillusioned with society. Neither Jack nor George understood or resonated with organized religion, leading them to purchase property northeast of Pittsburgh and establish a community with likeminded people.

Initially rooted in benign religious and hippie-like love and peace ideals, the group's nature began to change. After Jack's death in 1977, George assumed leadership, shifting the community's ethos toward a more rigorous doctrine and emphasizing the conversion of others.

Under George's influence, members bequeathed their life savings and insurance benefits to The Chosen, though their contributions essentially lined George's pockets. His children and grandchildren continued this legacy of financial manipulation.

Unlike their predecessors, the newer generation was a set of true believers in the cult's prophetic teachings of an impending war. Only the most fervent followers remained, and they discreetly recruited others of similar zeal.

Michelle's eyes widened. "Seriously?" She shook her head. "That is quite the coincidence, isn't it? Maybe the universe has conspired to have you two work together so you can finally bring The Chosen down."

"From your lips, sister." Journey blew out a long breath. Just thinking about The Chosen made her blood pressure rise. "I met Lucas briefly before I went undercover. After I came out of cover, we both helped the D.A. with the court case. I didn't know him well, but we weren't strangers."

"Ah." Michelle dropped her gaze to her plate.

Journey instantly knew she'd stuck her foot in her mouth. She'd been so focused on dishing about her partner that she hadn't considered the memories she'd be dredging up in the process.

It took only one look at Michelle's face for the memories to come up for Journey too.

Two years ago, Journey had been working undercover as

a member of The Chosen while Michelle lived in Chicago, working at the FBI field office there. She'd been doing well in her forensic analyst position before meeting a special agent who swept her off her feet.

Michelle's story didn't have a fairy-tale ending, though. Instead of being the good man any FBI agent should've been, Michelle's suitor kidnapped, sexually assaulted, and nearly killed her.

Journey still hated herself for not knowing what was happening in her sister's life back then. Sure, she'd been undercover at the time and had no way of knowing Michelle was missing, but Journey couldn't forgive herself for not knowing when Michelle had needed her most. It was only through sheer luck and willpower that she'd gotten to Chicago in time to help save her sister's life.

"I'm sorry." Journey dropped her fork and reached for Michelle's hand. "I didn't want to bring it up, but, full disclosure, I didn't want you to find out on your own. Figured you'd think I was hiding it from you."

Michelle's awkward smile said she was eager to change the subject. "Thank you."

Desperate to avoid saying something else, Journey shoved in a bite of chicken, and the explosion of flavor had her moaning with bliss. "This is incredible."

Thanks to Michelle's teaching, Journey could cook, too, but she'd never master the subtleties of the craft like her sister. This chicken piccata was melt-in-your-mouth delish.

"Aw, thanks." Michelle reached for the bread but paused and pulled her hand back as if she'd changed her mind. "I forgot we have muffins for dessert. Can't wait to try them. If the special agent thing doesn't work out, you could kill it as a baker."

Journey tapped her fork against her cheek. "Having a

sweet tooth is my secret to success." She finished chewing. "Hey, speaking of secrets. How's the new job going?"

Michelle's face brightened. She'd recently transferred onto the Evidence Response Team, ERT, from the forensic lab, where she'd been an analyst. If Journey had her way, she'd have her sister on every one of her cases.

"I love ERT. I admit, I didn't expect to enjoy being in the middle of the action so much. All the variety and the new challenges are so exciting." Michelle took a sip of tea.

Journey's cell buzzed in her pocket. For the first time in twenty-four hours, she was tempted to ignore the call. It'd been two years since Michelle's kidnapping, and with all the trauma that followed, Michelle was only now starting to act more up than down. If her sister was enjoying something, Journey wanted the full scoop.

"Just last week," Michelle launched into her story, "there was a case where the angle of a bank's CCTV couldn't capture the location of a shooter. I determined his probable location by assessing the bullet wipe, ballistics trajectory, and limiting factors within the shooting zone. The perp fired eight rounds, but only one hit its mark. He was a terrible shot."

"That's amazing. How—"

When the phone buzzed again, Journey gave in and pulled the device from her pocket to check the caller ID. This was a call she didn't have the luxury of letting go to voicemail.

"I want to hear more, but it's my partner. I've got to take it."

Michelle stabbed a bite of chicken, but a tiny twinkle entered her eye. "Man in Black calls."

"Har." Journey pressed the answer button and lifted the phone to her ear. "Hey, Lucas. What's up?"

"We got a call about a robbery and homicide at Faulkner's

Guns & Ammo. Kenner wants us to head to the crime scene." Lucas Sullivan had, of all things, a light Korean accent, despite his file indicating he grew up in the states. His Rs and Ls came out sounding a little bit the same. "The murder appears to be similar to that park ranger from West Virginia we were handed last week. Oh, and ATF is on scene too. Check in with Agent Blaine Dubovsky if you get there before me. Looks like there're quite a few weapons missing."

So much for hanging out with Michelle.

Journey sighed. "A dead ranger and missing guns? You couldn't possibly keep me away."

3

When Journey arrived at Faulkner's Guns & Ammo, she immediately spotted her new partner, Special Agent Lucas Sullivan, leaning his broad shoulders against the wall next to the front door. She'd barely had time to throw her hair into a messy bun. Meanwhile, Lucas was the picture of nonchalant cool with his black hair slicked back, not an ebony strand out of place, and his blue jeans and FBI windbreaker.

He was definitely giving off the James Dean vibes she'd described to Michelle earlier.

As Journey approached, police and ATF officers milled about the parking area while crime scene techs took photos and packaged evidence.

After regarding Journey a moment with eyes as cool and gray as wet stone, Lucas nodded toward the entrance. "Ready to head in?"

"Won't that wall fall down without you to hold it up?"

Now Lucas's eyebrows jumped upward as he pushed the door open, the corners of his mouth twitching. "Nothing could make me feel more important."

Journey covered a snort with her hand as they stepped

into the well-lit shop, where the cloying odors of gunpowder and oil choked the air.

Allegheny County had several firearms dealers, all clustered on the outskirts like this one. Though outside of the store was a nondescript cement, inside, Faulkner's was unique among its competition. In Journey's experience, most gun shops were cave-like and stuffed to the ceiling with stock. Faulkner's, however, featured clean shelves, white tile floors, white paneled walls. No junk. The only other colors in the room were the black and steel of the firearms.

Which made Sam Faulkner's body, splayed on the floor at the front counter with a large pool of blood around him, stand out like a horror display.

"With the right lighting in here, looks like a photo shoot." Journey stared at the macabre scene.

Lucas didn't have the chance to do more than nod before a guy with a face like a clean-scrubbed peach offered his hand.

"Special Agents Russo, Sullivan? I'm Agent Blaine Dubovsky, ATF. Police called us in, as per protocol, since this incident involves a firearms dealer."

Journey noted how Blaine's windbreaker still held the creases from the packaging, as if this were the first time he'd put it on. That with baby face and his hair so neatly styled, he looked about as green as you could get. The "as per protocol" didn't help.

Fresh out of training. Yikes. Journey crossed her fingers that her first case with her new partner wouldn't turn into a mess because of this greenie.

After they'd each shaken his hand, Lucas got the ball rolling. "Got the low-down for us?"

"Pittsburgh Zone One responded to a shots-fired call from a neighbor. Neighbor didn't enter premises, just heard the shots and reported. Guess he didn't want to get involved in a shoot-out in a gun shop."

"Smart witness." Journey scanned the shelves. There were enough firearms to arm a midsize country. She wouldn't want to be caught in that cross fire either.

"One of the local officers conducted the interview, should be in the file later tonight."

Blaine led Journey and Lucas to a gap-toothed display of semiautomatic handguns along the left side of the store.

Lucas let out a low whistle. "Could the perp have been more obvious?"

"Gotta wonder." Blaine hooked a thumb toward the front counter near the victim's body. "Faulkner appears to have been going over paperwork before the murder. From the looks of it, he liked things done a certain way. I'm hoping his inventory records are equally type A. That'll give us a jump on comparing what's physically in the store to what ought to be here."

"Fingers crossed."

Bending close but not touching the display, Journey examined the obvious gaps. "Has this area been cleared?"

"Yeah, it's—" When a crime scene tech bustled up, Blaine turned away to speak with her before excusing himself to follow her outside. "Let me know if you need anything."

After pulling on a pair of gloves, Journey flicked a switch on the display's side, lighting up the remaining firearms with a cold, white backlight. She leaned close, closing one eye. "Bolts are cut."

Wearing his own gloves, Lucas tried to jiggle the Ruger .380 bolted into the spot next to Journey's face. "Meaning the perp either brought a bolt cutter or bothered to get one from the back. If they brought their own, I'll give them points for preparedness."

"We'll have to look for any missing tools too. Here's

hoping this guy was type A about all his stuff." Journey's gaze shifted to the shop's front door, where she spotted Michelle heading toward the body. "If I'd known you'd be here, we could have carpooled."

"My cell rang when I got in the Mustang." Michelle plopped a sturdy case onto the floor. "But I had to pick up equipment, so it's better I drove myself."

"You two know each other?" Lucas extended a hand to Michelle. "I'm Lucas Sullivan."

"Lucas, this is my sister, Michelle Timmer." Journey cocked her head, eyeing Lucas's FBI windbreaker and jeans. "See, Michelle? My description of him was pretty good. He's looking very James Dean tonight. Though maybe a little less *Men in Black* in that outfit."

Michelle accepted Lucas's handshake. "Please excuse her. We were having dinner, and I asked about her new partner. I had nothing to do with the movie star references."

Lucas smiled. "I like James Dean. And Tommy Lee Jones."

Now Journey cocked her head Michelle's direction. "Michelle, however, looks like Abby Sciuto from *NCIS*. She's also a brilliant forensic scientist. But real-life brilliant."

"And I'm not so much into the goth look." Michelle gestured at her plain jeans and sweatshirt, then glanced toward a tall man advancing from across the room. "Here comes Dr. Simon."

Journey had worked with the forensic pathologist before. Dr. Smith Simon came with a stellar reputation for trustworthiness. But also, his name, consisting of a last name first and a first name last, amused her. Between that and a distinct Doc Brown look from *Back to the Future*, she struggled not to giggle when meeting his gaze.

Mercifully, Dr. Simon knelt beside the body to explain what he'd found so far.

"Single gunshot wound in the abdomen. Blunt force

trauma to the side of the head. Traumatic blow fractured the pterion, likely causing an epidural hematoma. That's where all that swelling is from. Notice how the left eye is bulging there."

Journey nodded. "Can't miss it. Poor guy."

"At first glance, it seems he might've bled out from this shot here." Dr. Simon pointed two fingers at the victim's belly. "There's certainly enough blood to have caused a significant drop in his blood pressure. But I have a hunch the blow to the head ruptured the middle meningeal artery, and that bleed, combined with the increased intracranial pressure, is what killed him. Of course, I'll know more once I have him on the table."

"Takes a good deal of force to fracture the skull, doesn't it?" Journey shot a glance at Michelle.

Before her sister could answer, Dr. Simon stood. "A well-placed strike can do quite a lot of damage. And this area here," he hovered a fingertip near Journey's temple, "is the weakest spot."

From where he still crouched next to the victim, Lucas tilted his chin up toward Dr. Simon. "Do we know what was used as a weapon for the blow?"

"If I had to guess, a rock. Probably no bigger than my fist. And jagged, based on the damage to the surrounding tissue. ACOME has some fragments they found near the body bagged up to for testing."

Simon was referring to the Allegheny County Office of the Medical Examiner. They had their own processing procedures, and hopefully, the lab would report back soon with any trace evidence the perp had been sloppy enough to leave behind.

Journey now understood what Lucas had meant when he'd first called her to the crime scene. This homicide was oddly similar to the one that had landed on their desk a week earlier. Though she couldn't see how a gun store owner in Pennsylvania and a park ranger in West Virginia were connected, they shared the same deadly wound patterns.

Her mind was already spinning, trying to puzzle it together.

And she still had an even bigger question…

"Other than the fact that both victims were shot and hit on the head with a rock, why do you think the murders are connected?"

Dr. Simon grinned. "Do you really think I'd have hauled you down here on a lovely Sunday evening with such a flimsy link?"

She grinned back. "I hope not."

Dr. Simon lifted a baggie containing a small glass bottle.

"What it is?" Journey squinted at the flakes inside.

"Blood. I found flakes both on the floor and inside the victim's head wound."

"Blood that doesn't match our victim?"

"Correct. I did a quick match of our victim's blood, and he's A positive. The flake is AB negative, which happens to be the rarest blood type in the U.S."

Excitement stirred in Journey's chest. "What's the park ranger's blood type?"

Simon winked at her. "AB negative." He held up a hand. "I know it's not enough to hang your hat on, but considering the types of wounds each victim sustained and the blood type coincidence, I thought it merited your attention."

Journey patted his arm. "You would be correct. How long before we can get a DNA match?"

He sighed. "You know the drill…twenty-four to forty-eight hours."

"But can't you run the rapid test?"

Simon gave her a withering look. "Why didn't I think of that?"

"Because I didn't remind you until just now." She patted his arm again, adding a comforting squeeze. "Sorry. But can you?"

"We'll see."

Officials had found the park ranger, Noah Hudson, dead inside a cabin he'd been assigned to prep for the upcoming camping season. The long winter had delayed the opening of many campsites in the national park by at least a month. That specific area wasn't designated for hunting, and weapons were prohibited there, but the borders between the national park and the designated hunting areas were a bit blurry.

Still, it wasn't even hunting season yet. And that campsite hadn't been fully opened to the public. Campers had only just begun to make reservations in the cabins for the season. There was no one in the area, and it wasn't until the ranger had failed to check in that anyone was aware of a problem. When they found his body, he had a single shot to the stomach and a nasty head wound.

If there was a connection between these two murders, she and Lucas would find it.

Michelle cleared her throat, drawing everyone's attention. She pointed toward a spot several feet away. "I was just over there with the local PD's crime scene tech examining a pistol they think is Faulkner's sidearm. Glock nineteen."

Lucas glanced in the tech's direction. "Discharged?"

"Once. There's a nine millimeter in the wall." Michelle pointed toward another tech examining a bullet hole.

Journey rubbed the gold ace of diamonds pendant hanging from her neck as her mind whirred, assembling the pieces of what they'd gathered so far. "So looks like Faulkner's in the shop. Presumably doing paperwork...alone. At some point, he's confronted. Gets off one shot."

"And judging from where his gun ended up, perp may have disarmed him." Lucas stood, but his gaze remained glued to the floor around the body.

Journey stepped back from Dr. Simon, angling toward Lucas. "Check out the rest of the scene?"

Lucas nodded.

From what the local PD and FBI teams had gathered so far, most of the activity happened in a small area at the front of the store. The area where Faulkner's body lay. The front doors showed no sign of forced entry, leaving speculation that the perp must have entered through the back.

However, crime scene techs said there were no marks on the rear entrance, either, and the lights were off when Pittsburgh officers arrived. Apparently the utilities company was called in to get the lights back up. The preliminary report mentioned a system virus.

"We'll need a list of everyone with access to a key or door codes." Journey jotted a reminder in her notebook.

"And copies of any background checks Faulkner had done on his team and anyone who might have had access to the shop." Lucas didn't look up from where he was adding notes to his own notebook.

Gun shops ran checks not only on the customers making a purchase but also on their employees. Per federal law, anyone with access to a lethal weapon necessitated a clean history. As such, gun shops also often ran checks on service providers, since the last thing an owner needed to worry about was an unstable personality in a store stocked floor to ceiling with deadly opportunity.

"No evidence of a missing tool, but..."

Journey had thought her muttering quiet enough, but Lucas still finished her thought aloud. "But that doesn't mean the perp didn't take anything after getting in."

"So it could still be an outsider." *Ugh.*

Michelle caught up with the agents a few minutes later. "Two things you ought to see." She led them back to the front counter. "Partial footprint. Here."

She pointed at a narrow strip of red, maybe two inches wide by three long. The tread was visible but smudged along the edge.

"And a handprint. Here." This time she pointed at the counter. A thick smear of blood swept across the surface next to the store's computer and phone—though neither appeared to have been touched. Nor had the stack of paperwork on the other side. A tumbler of something brown, bourbon or whiskey maybe, would need to be bagged and tested.

Michelle continued, "Unfortunately, it's mostly smudge. My hunch is, the perp was wearing some kind of nitrile gloves, as there were no fibers left behind."

Lucas leaned in for a closer look. "Didn't touch the mouse. Didn't touch the paperwork. Anything on the register or the drawers?"

Michelle shook her head. "Not so far as I know. I've been told by the techs working the back that the only thing disturbed was a stack of ammo cans on a shelf near the stockroom entrance. But neither the office nor break room was upended in any way. Files are neat. Cupboards don't appear to have been disturbed."

That fit with what the techs had told Journey and Lucas. "Wasn't hoping for cash, then." Journey knew if the perp had wanted both guns and money, they'd at least have rifled a few drawers. She made a mental note to ask if there was a safe in the office. "So the question is, did Faulkner get in the way of a simple firearms theft, or was he the target all along?"

4

Lucas Sullivan glanced at the glowing green numbers on the face of his watch.

Nine already, and still so much left to go over.

He made his way down the hallway toward the back office, beset on all sides by the low murmur of voices as crime scene techs worked every inch of the sales floor while Journey discussed the stolen weapons with ATF Agent Dubovsky.

The back offices were filled with a faint hum of activity, clinking of metal tools, and hushed conversation.

As he entered, Lucas spotted Pittsburgh Bureau of Police Detective Patty Traynor. She stood tall with a pencil-straight posture next to a low-profile server rack holding a monitor and keyboard on top.

Just the woman he was looking for. "Got anything?"

"Nothing of value, I'm afraid." Patty gave a swift head jerk that dislodged a few stray blond hairs from her tightly wound bun. Her gaze met his for a bare moment before returning to the racks, giving Lucas the distinct impression she was a no-nonsense kind of detective. "It appears Mr.

Faulkner's security system was somehow disabled when the perp came into the shop."

Lucas noted the dome camera in the upper corner of the ceiling. It was one of those elaborate setups with 4K night vision, thermal detection, and local storage. The server rack next to Patty, however, lacked flashing lights on one unit.

Faulkner sprang for an expensive setup. And it should've been worth every penny. So how did it fail?

"Any theories on how the perp managed that?" Lucas jotted down a quick note to research the specific model of the system later.

"Not that I can guess." Patty's shoulders slumped as she let out a defeated sigh. "These systems are pretty elaborate with app-enabled access and the keypads at the doors. But even if the perp had a code to get in, that wouldn't have shut the whole system down. Going to have to see what the computer guys say about it."

"If you haven't already," Lucas clicked his pen closed, "we should get a team out to check with the other businesses in this strip mall. Maybe they'll have surveillance footage of the back alley we can use."

"Already on it." She nodded. "Uniformed officers went out a few minutes before you came back here."

After thanking her, Lucas headed back to the hallway, turning over questions he couldn't yet answer and clues that didn't seem to add up.

The victim, Sam Faulkner, wasn't just careful about his paperwork. He had a backup system for every backup system. A gas-powered generator in case the electricity went out. Security lights. Silent alarm buttons at several locations throughout the shop. Most dealers only kept one near the cash register.

Was the guy more careful than his competitors, or did he have reason to be paranoid?

Lucas's ten years in the FBI's White-Collar Crime Unit had presented case study after case study in type A criminality, and Faulkner's exceptional attention to detail got his intuition tingling. In his experience, criminals who left the most damage in their wakes also structured their enterprises with extensive checks and balances, every measure designed to ensure the continuation of their schemes for years, if not decades.

They kept duplicate sets of books, avoided electronic communication, employed lawyers who knew every federal and state regulation. They placed cronies in all the right positions of power and influence. They surreptitiously and generously bought loyalty and silence to enable their crimes.

A careful business owner like Faulkner, with his multiple fail-safes, harbored one fear. A breach. No firearms dealer wanted to fall victim to their own wares. That much was obvious. And yet, most secured themselves and their cash with far less overhead.

Not so for Sam Faulkner. With all those precautions, his security had still somehow failed him.

Lucas meandered into Sam's empty office, scanning the area. The crime scene techs had already finished working the room without finding much. No prints. Nothing indicating a burglary. The safe was undisturbed. The chairs, one behind the desk and two facing it, remained upright. On Faulkner's desk, Lucas found a clean, white coffee mug that read, *My Dad's a Superhero*.

On the window ledge stood three framed photos. In one, Sam Faulkner and a woman with soft wrinkles around her eyes, presumably his wife, stood on a beach at sunset. They wore leis around their necks and had bright-red sunburns on their faces. Hawaii, most likely.

Next to that sat a family photo. Sam and his wife stood

behind two elementary-aged girls. Proud parents with their hands gently resting on their girls' shoulders.

Lucas's stomach tightened. They were young, but there was no age *old enough* to lose a father.

He straightened himself and attempted to clear his head.

Despite Lucas's efforts, Hallie's face drove its way front and center in his mind, hijacking his thoughts. *"Don't leave me, Dad."* His daughter's voice called out as tears soaked her cheeks.

"Not now." Lucas pressed a fist against his eye socket and pushed, needing the physical sensation, desperate to trick his brain out of its haunted spiral. Hallie was at home with her mom, Serena, his ex-wife. Probably hunched over her textbooks and doing geometry homework. Calculating the sides of an equilateral triangle inscribed in a circle. He'd been helping her with it last week.

"No, Dad. Please. Don't go!"

It wasn't the real Hallie agitating him, though. The voice was hers, but the words crying out in his mind—that was his own trauma. His inner child speaking through the guilt Lucas associated with co-parenting and late hours on the job.

He stood still for a long moment, fiddling with the clasp on his watch while he tamed his thoughts back into peaceful complicity.

"Focus on the items Faulkner left behind." The first two pictures had come with the sad new reality of a father gone too soon. The third, however, sent a jolt of recognition through Lucas. Sam Faulkner, in orange hunting gear from head to toe, stood next to a man Lucas knew.

Bryce Faulkner.

Sam and Bryce are related.

Lucas had put Bryce away for embezzlement. He was a member of a group called The Chosen, a cult that earned its money through theft and murder. The cult supplied the Feds with no shortage of atrocities to investigate, but so far, Bryce's had been the only case to make it all the way to a conviction.

Bryce hadn't been one of the murderous Righties. His crime was greed, pure and simple. He'd used his position as the accountant for a small Pittsburgh business to embezzle money and funnel it to The Chosen. Prosecutors had him dead to rights and offered him a reduced sentence in exchange for information that would help them secure the arrest and conviction of his superiors.

It was a damn good deal, but Bryce turned it down.

Right this minute, he was sitting in a cell and serving a ten-year sentence at FCI Elkton, a federal correctional institution just over the western border of Pennsylvania in Ohio.

This has to be something.

"Hey, Russo." Lucas hustled toward the front of the store, where he found Journey examining the bullet hole in the wall. "I think maybe it's time to go visit Sam's wife."

He gave her the rundown of his discovery. The neat-as-a-pin office. The over-the-top redundancies in Sam's security. And the brother sitting in prison for embezzlement.

Journey patted her jacket pocket, checking for her cell phone and keys. "I'll drive."

5

Nestled in an upper working-class neighborhood, the Faulkners' redbrick, single-story house overlooked a quiet, tree-lined street. Journey had grown up in Allegheny County and knew the area well. It had decent schools attended by the children of small business owners, making it a perfect place for their family.

The residence contrasted with the neighboring homes for the meticulousness of its care. Just like at the gun shop, everything was neat and tidy to the nth degree. Even in the dark, the lines of a fresh trim stood out on the manicured lawn. The bushes, too, all boasted perfect uniformity as they framed the path leading up to the front door.

"Any thoughts on how you want to approach this?" Journey pulled up to the curb and killed the ignition. She'd parked just beyond the view of the front window—the Faulkners had been through enough without having to worry about why the FBI was sitting outside their house.

Lucas unbuckled. "Police spoke with Mrs. Tammie Faulkner at length about an hour ago. Had an officer assigned to remain with the family, but the widow asked him to leave so she and the girls could grieve in peace. Officer says she's devastated but cooperative."

"Did she have any theories on what might've happened?"

He shook his head as he opened the car door. "Let's go find out."

A small, round porch light hung above the entrance, illuminating their approach. Mrs. Faulkner opened the door before either of them could knock, glaring at them with red, puffy eyes as she pulled her blanket around her shoulders. Her voice was hoarse. "I thought I said no more officers tonight."

A higher, more anxious voice called from farther in the house before Journey could introduce herself and Lucas. "Mom? Who's there?"

"My daughters and I are trying to have some quiet together. It's been..." Fresh tears streaked her cheeks, finishing her statement.

Journey fought the impulse to wrap an arm around Mrs. Faulkner's shoulder as she introduced herself and Lucas. "We're working in tandem with the Pittsburgh Bureau of Police investigating your husband's murder, and we'd like to ask you a few questions about what we found."

Fear widened Mrs. Faulkner's eyes, and Journey mentally kicked herself for her all-business approach. She'd been told she often came over a bit too mechanical at first greeting.

Lucas must've realized her mistake too. "I'm sorry. This must be alarming, especially given everything you're going through. We're trying to find your husband's killer. We want to understand why this happened. I'm sure you'd like those same answers, too, wouldn't you?"

Mrs. Faulkner studied them for a moment, then waved them into the house. "Make yourselves comfortable. Be right back. I need to speak with my girls. Don't want them getting all riled up with more worry."

To Journey's relief, the inside of the Faulkner home showed off a more feminine touch. She could respect Sam's penchant for order, but not everyone could relax in a family room straight off the pages of a magazine. In contrast to the shop, the house gave off color, vitality. Gingham curtains. Floral throw pillows. A wicker basket full of magazines.

Journey surveyed her seating options, eyeing a spot on the couch next to Lucas. She didn't love the two-against-one look, but it could be the best option.

Choosing a seat was always tricky business. She preferred an angle from which she could make easy eye contact with everyone but not be so close as to invade their host's space. Though if she were too far away from Mrs. Faulkner, she risked appearing cold and unsympathetic, chilling the conversation.

Lucas had plopped himself down without hesitation, raising his eyebrow at her reluctance to sit. "I don't bite."

"So you claim." She sat next to him and glanced at the family photo on the side table. In it, the girls were teenagers and near carbon copies of their mother. Both were slender with brown, shoulder-length hair. According to Lucas's briefing on the way over, Renee was sixteen years old, and Angie was thirteen. Sam had owned the gun shop for twelve years. Tammie, his wife, was a nurse at a senior living facility.

Mrs. Faulkner returned, settling into a chair facing them. "Can we please make this quick? I've had about all I can take for one day."

"Of course, ma'am." Journey took the lead. "First, and this is only for timeline purposes, can you tell us about your whereabouts and actions over the last twenty-four hours?"

For a moment, it looked like Mrs. Faulkner would protest. But she closed her eyes, took a deep breath, and detailed getting up, going to church, baking cookies with her daughters, and calling her mother. A fairly typical day.

Except for the husband-getting-murdered part. "Is that a good enough rendition?"

"Yes, ma'am. Now we can move on." Lucas offered a disarming, sheepish smile.

Mrs. Faulkner, who'd shown signs of possible hostility, gave a tiny smile back.

Lucas pulled out his phone and showed her the picture of Sam and Bryce he'd found at the store. "This is your brother-in-law, Bryce Faulkner, correct?"

Mrs. Faulkner frowned at the image. "Yes, it is."

"And Bryce is currently serving a sentence at FCI Elkton, having been convicted of embezzlement?"

She sighed and nodded, rubbing her eyes with the heels of her hands. "He sure is."

"Mrs. Faulk—"

"Call me Tammie, please."

"Tammie." Lucas leaned forward, his face intent. "Can you tell us what you know about Bryce and his affiliation with The Chosen?"

Journey appreciated Lucas holding back mentioning their involvement in the investigation leading to her brother-in-law's conviction. He was probably betting that the less he and Journey appeared to understand about Bryce, the more Tammie might offer.

"I don't know much. Sam never liked those righteous bastards." Tammie shrugged, knocking her blanket off one shoulder. "That's what he called them. And because he didn't like to talk about them, I tried to avoid the subject as much as possible. He loved his brother, and I think it really upset him to see Bryce get mixed up in all that."

Bastards is right.

Journey knew all too well what that organization was about. For eight months, she'd posed as a new and eager member, quickly gaining clout with the group thanks to an

FBI informant on the inside. The Bureau followed her so-called indoctrination, and her work helped them trace swindled funds through The Chosen's sham tax dodging and Ponzi schemes.

Though there were some true believers. Connor Leopold, grandson of The Chosen's co-founder, believed he was an angel born into the body of a man and brought to earth to spread word of an upcoming war between believers and nonbelievers.

Under Connor's direction, she and her fellow members stockpiled canned goods in the community kitchen. Split firewood. Made quilts. Rolled bandages.

They were dispatched to street corners with pamphlets and invitations to a new kind of church. She hawked the group's miracle wellness drink, even though it was nothing more than off-brand Kool-Aid, repackaged and sold at exorbitant prices. Most of all, Journey was taught to pressure fellow members into taking out gigantic life insurance policies and designating The Chosen as the beneficiary.

Journey did so herself. With the Bureau's help, she signed over a $500,000 policy. The goal was to track it, see if cult leaders tried to take a lien against the funds. Little did they suspect that, less than a month later, a member would ambush Journey in the middle of the night and put a knife to her throat.

Goose bumps crawled up the back of Journey's neck every time she thought of the two near-death experiences she'd endured because of The Chosen. First, they'd burned down her house. Then they'd sent someone to kill her for a life insurance policy scheme. She'd managed to survive both attacks, but she'd never uncovered solid proof The Chosen was responsible.

Thinking of the assassin so committed to The Chosen as to try to kill her, Journey made a mental note to tread carefully with her next line of questioning. "Can you tell us more about their relationship?"

"Sam refused to give up on Bryce." Tammie's posture stiffened. "The rest of the family eventually cut ties. They couldn't deal with the embarrassment of all that cult business. The Faulkners aren't the most forgiving people. And they weren't interested in listening to him or explaining Bryce's affiliation to anyone else." She hugged the blanket closer. "Sam, though. He always kept trying. He made sure Bryce knew he was welcome at our house anytime. If he reached out, Sam was there for him."

Journey glanced at her notes. "Did that openness extend to his brother's involvement with The Chosen as well?"

"Definitely not." Tammie scoffed. "Like I said, Sam didn't like to talk about The Righties. He told me once that Bryce tried to convince him to go to his church. But when Sam made his mind up about something, he almost never backed down. Bryce knew better than to waste his breath."

Lucas shifted in his seat and cleared his throat, appearing uncomfortable. Journey thought he might be trying a tactic she often found effective—waiting for the moment to settle before changing topics. "Let's jump forward to Bryce's trial, okay?"

Tammie let out a breath and settled back in her chair. "Yeah, that was rough."

"Hard on Sam, you mean?"

"Hard on everyone. By then, the girls were old enough to understand their uncle was in serious trouble. He was on the news. How could we keep it from them? And then there was the teasing, of course."

Journey nodded, watching Tammie closely. "From kids at school?"

"Sure, they'd all heard about 'The Righties.'" Tammie air-quoted the words. "Everyone in this area has. Some of the middle school boys used to call Angie 'culty' in the hallways. It upset her so badly that her older sister, Renee, finally came to us about it. And we had to explain that, yes, their uncle was a part of this group we didn't understand, but that didn't make him a bad person. Of course, that did little to stop those bullies at school."

The memory deflated Tammie further, if that was possible. She leaned her head back against the chair and closed her eyes for a moment. Journey and Lucas gave her the pause.

"The thing I could never understand," Tammie let out a deep sigh, "is how Bryce got wrapped up in a group like that to begin with. He was smart. He had a good job. Sam seemed confident he'd come to his senses one day. Get out of there."

Journey nodded as she listened to Tammie talk, giving her plenty of time to answer without interruption.

"But then, after the conviction," Tammie dropped her gaze to the carpet, "Sam admitted that may have been wishful thinking on his part. Bryce was making too much money to leave, which seemed to matter to him a lot. Those brothers grew up dirt poor with a daddy who only showed his love with his fists. Suddenly, Bryce has a decent salary, plus access to his employer's accounts. He and Sam were different in a lot of ways, but neither one ever liked to have his back against the wall. Physically, financially, or otherwise."

Journey suspected the FBI knew more about Bryce's crimes than Sam or Tammie ever found out. He'd embezzled a half-million dollars, the vast majority of which went directly to The Chosen.

"Whatever Bryce stole, he didn't spend on himself." Tammie leaned forward in her chair as if to make sure they'd heard her statement clearly. "He gave the girls lovely birthday and Christmas gifts, but he just about burst a gasket when Sam and I flew to Hawaii for our anniversary. Called the trip lavish. Accused Sam of getting too big a head."

Lucas shot a side-eye at Journey. "I saw a picture in Sam's office of the two of you on the beach at sunset. Was that the same trip?"

Fresh tears welled in Tammie's eyes. "Yeah."

Journey raised an eyebrow, intrigued. "Did they ever resolve the argument?"

"The storm passed eventually." Tammie waved a dismissive hand in the air. "But each of them was as bullheaded as the other. Bryce had his opinions, and Sam had his. Only, Sam was the younger of the two. Bryce would never change his beliefs on account of his little brother."

Feeling like she had gleaned all the information she could from this topic, Journey switched to the list of standard questions they needed answers to. Alibis. Financials. The state of their marriage. Friends. Enemies. Threats. Even when the questions got personal, Tammie seemed to answer them honestly.

"Thank you, Tammie." Journey placed her business card on the table. "We appreciate you taking the time to speak with us tonight."

After weighing all they'd learned tonight, Journey concluded their investigation didn't need to bother Tammie any further. If someone had planned Sam Faulkner's murder, it didn't appear to be his wife. Which left them where they'd started—with a dead body, missing guns, and no suspects.

6

Journey tossed and turned, her mind racing from all the unknowns of the case and the similarity of the two homicides, despite having occurred miles apart. And if that weren't enough, the shadows of forgotten memories crept up from the depths of her subconscious. She remained entrenched in her blankets, determined to beat insomnia, but the maelstrom of unwanted and chaotic thoughts made sleep impossible.

Her alarm went off at six a.m., forcing her to admit defeat.

Resigning to her fate, Journey pushed back the duvet and stepped onto the cold wooden floor. The tile in her bathroom made her shiver as she went through her morning ritual. Wanting nothing more than to crawl back into bed, she splashed her face with water and pulled her hair into a ponytail so tight the fine lines that had begun to show next to her eyes smoothed out.

Dracula yowled impatiently from his place beside his food bowl, demanding to be fed as Journey shuffled into the living room. His green eyes glowed against his silky black fur, reflecting the dim morning light from the window.

"Yeah, yeah. I hear you." She blearily reached for a can of salmon pâté, silencing her demanding cat with a wet plop of ground-up meat into his bowl, before hopping on the treadmill.

The rhythm of her feet pounding against the belt soothed her rattled mind. This was her happy place, a sanctuary where each stride released a cascade of endorphins that provided her with an escape from all the negative thoughts normally filling her mind.

Dracula jumped up on the handrail and began to lick his paw. He'd become part of her little family shortly after she'd returned to Pennsylvania, where she picked him up from a shelter. As a stray who'd lost his original family, Dracula needed someone reliable to come home to. Just like Journey. They'd been the perfect fit for each other.

"You're my person, aren't you, Drac?"

He lowered his paw and gazed up at her. His eyes seemed to hold an age-old wisdom, making Journey sometimes wonder if her cat truly was a reincarnation of the famous vampire.

Prrrup.

She smiled at the half purr, half meow. Journey decided that was a yes and gave him a good scratching behind the ears for exactly five seconds. A second longer, and she'd get swatted.

While Dracula curled up on her bed for a well-deserved, post-breakfast nap, Journey took a quick shower, threw her hair up into a messy bun, and made it to the office before seven.

She entered the FBI field office and made her way to the fourth floor, where rows of workstations in the bullpen stretched out from the elevator like a windowless city.

Fingers clattered on keyboards, phones rang from various desks, and papers flapped while agents sorted through mountains of paperwork.

Special agent hours were rarely nine to five, so it was no surprise to Journey when she spotted Lucas already at his desk—or in this case, their desks. They'd pushed two together in the back corner of the bullpen, forming a makeshift pod, so they could face each other.

Journey smiled as she took her seat at the desk directly opposite him. "You a restless sleeper like me, or am I working with an early bird now?"

Lucas slid a cup of takeout coffee across the mega-desk. "Is seven o'clock early now?" He chuckled, taking a sip from his own cup. "Couldn't turn the brain off, is all."

"My hero." Journey gulped the dark, extra-hot coffee and sighed as its warmth trickled its way down her throat. "I remembered to feed the cat but somehow forgot I needed a fresh infusion of caffeine to get my brain going."

He snorted. "We'll need every brain cell today."

"Not that I mind..." She set down the cup and regarded her partner across the desk. "But why are you always so generous?"

"Holdover from my first partner." Lucas shifted his weight back in his chair and shrugged. "He never brought coffee. Even if he was picking some up for himself, he never offered. Not that he was a bad guy. Outstanding agent. I just decided I'd rather be a different sort of partner."

Lucas's disappointments were Journey's gain. So far, she'd had decent partners, even though none of them had kept her buzzing with caffeine. She lifted her cup with a smile. "Here's to being partners in coffee."

They air-toasted.

Journey leaned forward, keeping her voice to a whisper.

"For future, totally unrelated reference...how do you take yours?"

Lucas grinned. "Darkest roast available. Two sugars. No cream."

She made a mental note and settled in at her desk. Before leaving the house, she'd wrapped a yellow scarf around her neck, forever striving to add a dash of color to a closetful of dull navy, black, and gray suits. Now, though it was still a chilly April morning, the silk felt hot and clingy against her neck. She pulled at it, tempted to toss it in the trash.

Today was going to be one of those days. "No autopsy report yet, I take it?" Journey started typing her password in, ready to get down to business.

"None that I've seen." Lucas moved to his computer and began typing. "I was going to dig around in the Bryce Faulkner case notes this morning. See if there's anything about the cult I'm forgetting."

Journey gritted her teeth. Spending most of her time tossing and turning instead of getting sleep was because of her mind spiraling over The Chosen.

When she was young and growing up in Allegheny County, her parents' best friends had become some of The Righties. Eventually, they'd grown disillusioned with the never-ending requests for money. And after they were coerced into taking out a large life insurance policy with The Chosen as beneficiary, they wanted out. Her parents tried to help them leave.

Then both households burned to the ground at the same time, an unimaginable loss for Journey. Her parents and younger sister, Elaine, were gone in a single night, while she escaped because she'd sneaked out to meet a boy at the park.

Most people would have never let The Chosen enter their thoughts after a loss like that.

Not Journey.

Years later, she eagerly accepted an opportunity to go undercover with the cult for the Bureau. She was stationed in Las Vegas at the end, on the verge of marrying the wrong man. Discovering he was doing his own kind of undercover work, investigating the anatomy of another woman, was a blessing in disguise.

Journey dumped the guy, but since they were both FBI, she couldn't avoid him. Taking the undercover assignment gave her the chance to investigate The Chosen's connection to the fiery, suspiciously coincidental deaths of her family and her parents' friends. Bonus, she wouldn't have to deal with her ex anymore, making the decision even easier.

For eight months, Journey lived and breathed The Chosen, but in the end, she'd wound up with a knife at her throat and no answers to her questions about her history. Still, she'd done her part to blow most of the cult to smithereens and hoped to put all of that behind her. Yet now, here she was again, landing a case with a loose but not insignificant tie back to The Chosen.

Would she have to deal with them, in one way or another, for the rest of her life?

Journey needed a distraction from the downward spiral of her thoughts. "What did we learn last night?"

Lucas swiveled around to face her. "I keep going back to the fact that Bryce never rolled on The Chosen. Did he know about their penchant for murder? Because if he did, it's easy to understand why he stayed quiet."

Journey *hmm*ed. "Keep in mind he exposed them regardless. Just by getting caught."

"You suspect killing Sam could've been an act of revenge?"

Possibly. Though she didn't have evidence to back up the theory.

Journey shrugged. "Just throwing it out there. But if that's the case for Sam, how does it tie back to Noah Hudson, the park ranger from last week?"

"I couldn't say. Hudson was squeaky clean. A boy scout, all grown up." Lucas stood and paced the perimeter of their corner. "With Sam Faulkner, however, we have a thread to pull on. Maybe Faulkner's death wasn't a delayed reaction to his brother's troubles. What if it was the culmination of Sam's interaction with The Chosen?"

"Tell me more." Journey hadn't worked that closely with Lucas on Bryce's case back when he was with White Collar Crimes, but she remembered the sharp razor of his mind and his fondness for detail.

"Tammie said that 'to her knowledge,'" Lucas air-quoted, "Sam wanted nothing to do with them."

"You're thinking he was involved with The Chosen somehow but kept it from her?"

Lucas pivoted on his heel, switching directions. "Possibly."

"And perhaps those interactions weren't by choice."

"Right. We've got a dead gun shop owner and a yet-to-be-determined number of missing firearms." Lucas counted on his fingers as he continued to pace. "They tried to kill you for a life insurance policy. What threats would they make to Sam in exchange for a limitless supply of guns?"

Goose bumps raced up Journey's neck again. "And who needs guns more than an army preparing for war?" Who knew how many hours she'd spent listening to The Chosen's leaders go on about visions of the last battle? They'd pounded the word *war* into their followers' every waking thought.

Lucas abruptly stopped pacing. "I really hope none of what we're theorizing turns out to be true."

Journey raised her coffee. "I'll drink to that."

He only nodded. "Cheers."

"Here's a crazy thought." Journey finished her coffee and tossed the cup in the garbage. "We could sit here in the office speculating about Bryce Faulkner pulling Sam into The Chosen, or we could invite ourselves over to his place for a face-to-face."

"FCI Elkton is only an hour away." Lucas reached for his car keys. "I may or may not have mapped it on the GPS this morning."

"And I may or may not let you drive…on one condition." Journey held up a finger with a sly grin. "We have to stop for more coffee on the way."

7

They arrived at Federal Correctional Institution Elkton a little after ten. Journey had called ahead, and once they finished the check-in process and passed through security, the visiting room officer ushered them to a cramped concrete box they used as a private conference room.

While private, the windowless room was the size of a compact car with bottom-of-the-line amenities. Steel chairs. A cement table. Whitewashed brick walls.

Bryce Faulkner hadn't aged well. Gray hair was to be expected of a man in his early fifties, but deep bags under his eyes and the yellowing skin that sagged over the collar of his jumpsuit weren't.

Though Bryce turned his attention to Journey first, before she could get out a word, Lucas took the lead. "We'd like to ask you a few questions about your relationship with The Chosen. Since your conviction, what sort of communication have you had with any of its members or leadership?"

Journey didn't like the way Lucas stole the lead, jumping on Bryce in a turn-the-tables tactic the moment he tried to single her out. She made a mental note to call him out on it later.

"*Communication* is a fancy word for what happens in this place, Special Agent Sullivan." Bryce leaned back in his chair and put an ankle over the opposite knee.

"Call it what you like." Lucas maintained his neutral expression. "Have you heard from them?"

Bryce smirked. "A card every Christmas and a chocolate egg with my name on it for Easter."

"Any visitors? Maybe money deposited into your canteen account?" There were millions of small ways to connect with an inmate. Lucas kept up his intense round of questions. "Messages through fellow inmates? A guard who somehow knows all the same people as you?"

"Why the hell would I have anything to do with that herd of ass clowns?" Bryce's lip curled into a sneer. "They landed me here." He scoffed and pitched forward in his seat. "And money? Oh, yeah. They're known worldwide for their generosity. Didn't you hear about the defense attorney they hired for my trial?"

Bryce had been given a public defender after The Chosen abandoned him.

Lucas shot Journey an inquiring glance. Time for the good cop to step up.

She leaned forward, her voice low and calm. "But you didn't flip on them. Even after they left you to fend for yourself. If that were me, I'd be feeling disloyal or at least ready to give the government something in exchange for less time in here." She motioned toward the dreary gray and cold steel of their surroundings. "Or better amenities."

Bryce flashed her a smile and a wink. "Aren't you cute? All your thinkin'?"

Journey gave him her best ain't-I-precious smile. She enjoyed when convicts underestimated her tenacity. "I'm not the one wasting away in here, wearing a faded brown institution uniform and stinking like last night's stroganoff."

Lucas let out a barely audible chuckle.

Bryce's expression hardened into a glare. "And you wonder why I got no interest in helping the government?"

Journey shrugged. "You're smart enough to help yourself. But if you spend too much time trying to figure out which way the wind is blowing, you'll miss your chance."

She sat back in her seat, mimicking Bryce's earlier cocky body language, and let him stew with his thoughts. If he were a smart man, he'd decide to play ball. But Journey doubted he'd do the right thing.

Time stretched out as the tension dissipated, but Bryce remained quiet.

Journey would have preferred to bite her tongue off than be the first to break the silence. She was a little disappointed with Lucas when he caved first. "Well, as much as I'm enjoying all the valuable information you've enlightened us with," Lucas cleared his throat, "we've got some news of our own to share with you...about your brother, Sam."

Bryce's face brightened. "He here with you?"

"Not in the physical sense, strictly speaking."

"What?" Bryce leaned forward, placing his hands on the table.

"Sam Faulkner was found dead on the floor of his gun store last night." Lucas paused, allowing the gravity of what he'd said to sink in. "He'd sustained a shot to the gut and a skull-crushing blow to the head."

The more Journey worked with Lucas, the more she liked his style. Sometimes shock was the best way to fish for a reaction. Admittedly, she wouldn't have gone for that severe of an information drop. But it seemed to have hit the right mark.

Bryce sat in stunned silence, blinking as his mouth gaped.

"What we're wondering," Lucas softened his tone, "is if Sam's death had anything to do with the people who left you in here to rot—"

Bryce exploded from his seat. "You're lying. Get out of here. Just stop talking. I don't want to hear your bullshit lies." His knees buckled, and Bryce dropped back into the chair.

"Wish I was lying." Lucas sent a glance Journey's way, asking her to chime in and corroborate his story.

"I know it's a lot to process." Journey struggled for the right words to say. She needed an emotional edge to prod Bryce into revealing what he knew. "If it's any consolation, we checked on Tammie and the girls. They were grieving, obviously, but all three of them were safe at home. At least, for now. But if The Chosen is involved—"

"No way." Sweat beaded on Bryce's brow, and tiny droplets rained down on the table as he shook his head. "They were greedy sons of bitches, but they weren't killers."

Journey, of all people, knew that wasn't true. The Chosen had tried to kill her for her life insurance. Sent one of their soldiers into her apartment in the middle of the night. She'd fought him off in hand-to-hand combat all too reminiscent of her fiercest days at Quantico.

But despite knowing the truth, she held her tongue. If The Chosen was behind Sam Faulkner's murder, they needed a motive, and so far, Bryce hadn't coughed up so much as a hint of one.

Bryce turned his face to the wall, as if that would hide the tears leaking from the edges of his eyes. "The Feds killed my brother. You're in here trying to get me to squeal when you ought to be looking at yourselves. 'Those who hath power will fight to the death before giving it up.'"

Journey recognized one of the rallying cries of The Chosen against the evil government overlords.

"Think about it." Lucas met Bryce's fire with his own.

"When you got caught, you put The Righties in the government's crosshairs. No more hiding. Because of you, every penny The Chosen takes in gets scrutinized. Leopold can't be thrilled with you. That's my guess. But you're locked up. So who do they go after? Your brother, Sam."

Bryce was having none of it. "No. They'd have gotten to me. They'd have found a way. Sam had nothing to do with this."

Journey watched Bryce's reaction closely, studying every micro-expression. Sweat dripped down his brow as he clasped onto the words of his prophet for solace, blaming the Feds, an enemy The Chosen had taught him to hate, for Sam's death.

He was angry with the cult that had left him alone to pay for its misdeeds, and still The Chosen somehow controlled Bryce's thoughts. She didn't see a man realizing he'd made an irreparable mistake. Instead, she witnessed a sad and crazed brother who felt he had no place to turn.

If he gave them any useful information, it wouldn't happen today.

Journey nodded toward the door.

Lucas pushed his chair back, but didn't stand right away. "I'll leave you with this to consider. We're not stopping until we find out who killed Sam. We owe it to him and his family. And I think you believe that too. You've got plenty to be pissed about, sure. You let yourself get used, and now you're here, paying the price. So hate us. Hate the Feds. Hate the cult. I can't change that. But I saw the look in your eyes when you heard Sam was dead. When you're ready to do whatever it takes to get justice for your little brother, let us know."

Standing, Lucas knocked on the window, signaling to the visiting room officer that they were finished.

For now.

8

Killing was almost too easy. Like a reflex, once the adrenaline kicked in. A few simple twitches of muscle. Planning had been the hard part. All the plotting, observing, and acting with precision. Everything had to be perfect. No mistakes.

My first kill had gone better than I could've hoped. A practice run to make sure I wouldn't lose my nerve. It was one thing to take a ten-point buck down. Shooting a man in cold blood and bashing their skull in...that was the true test of my resolve. And watching the light leave their eyes was surprisingly satisfying.

After I'd proved my mettle, taking out that park ranger in West Virginia, I was confident I could accomplish my other goals. I'd anticipated the ranger being my most difficult quarry. The man had been an outdoorsman for almost a decade. Taking him out first meant the others would be uncomplicated by comparison.

He'd been shockingly easy to hunt and eliminate.

Surprise was the ultimate advantage, it turned out.

Sam Faulkner was the second name I checked off my list.

He'd always acted as if having a gun in his hand made him untouchable.

I showed him.

Euphoric energy filled my body as I drove to the storage unit where Mother waited. She was going to be so proud of me.

"Justice is done."

She beamed. I adored the way excitement filled her eyes. All I wanted to do was make her happy and see that smile.

"The job was easier than I thought." I sprang the padlock on my storage unit and rolled the door open. Inside, there was plenty of room for my new treasures, including a gun safe standing in the corner, waiting to be filled.

"I told you it would be."

"Sam thought his shop was impenetrable." I snorted a laugh. "But his security system was a joke. A directional antenna and RF transceiver were all it took to open the back door. Sam didn't know I was in the building until I was ready to make my move."

Mother didn't shift to help as she watched from the doorway, assessing my loot as I unloaded the trunk. "Most of what you grabbed are semiautomatics, I see. Good choice."

"They'll be worth more if I decide to sell them, don't you think?"

"Absolutely." She gave me a satisfied nod.

"I didn't forget the ammunition either." I held up a box for her to see. "Practically cleaned Sam out before leaving."

"Making justice look like a robbery gone wrong." She pressed her hands to her chest, as if needing to hold in a heart grown too big to fit. "You are so brilliant."

My spirits soared at Mother's praise. "The way I figure, cops will focus on all the wrong evidence. They'll be working on finding a thief willing to murder anyone who tries to stop them from stealing. No real motive to follow. Just the tragic death of someone trying to play hero to save their stuff from being stolen. It's perfect in its simplicity and will keep law enforcement chasing their tails long after I've completed my list."

As I loaded in the last of the boxes, I wondered if I should make each murder look like a bungled burglary attempt. Keep law enforcement busy chasing after their favorite suspects rather than getting wise to any links between the crimes. At least until I crossed everyone off my list and sent them all to rot in Hell.

Mother must've read my mind. "You look so focused and sure of yourself. After last night, there's no doubt. You were born for this. It's your purpose."

Her words stunned me. "What do you mean?"

"Don't you see it?" Mother's voice was gentle but held a distinct note of certainty. "How brilliantly you performed. Imagine how much wrong you could set right again in this sad, demented world."

"Isn't that exactly what I'm already doing?"

"Yes. Because those people deserve to die." Her eyes glimmered with unshed tears. "But you have to think bigger. You were born to bring justice. For yourself. For me. For everything our family lost."

I hung my head. "I know."

Her softness turned hard with anger. She balled her wrinkled hands into fists. "But the injustice doesn't end with us. Do you think we're the only ones who've suffered at the hands of the evil in this world? That we're the last ones to have been victims of a crime, only to be victimized again when the law did nothing? They profess to protect and serve, but they did nothing to punish the guilty. You've done more in the last week to bring us closure than any officer of the law."

She frightened me when she got this angry. I was only

one person. I'd warned her I couldn't absolve every evil in the world, but she'd lost track of that, become single-minded and bent on revenge disguised as justice.

Arguing only made it worse. I held my tongue, determined not to anger her further.

Mother stepped closer and looked deep into my eyes. "You are the one who can exact justice and bring peace. You have it within you. Look at the good you've already done. There's more, but you have to accept it as your calling...with all your heart."

The one.

Though I know she only meant to keep me from wavering, her words echoed in the air like a revelation, and my heart swelled with pride. She was right.

I had proved I could do what was needed. I was the one bringing justice to our family. Why not do it for others?

"You're right." I lifted my chin and met her gaze, my decision made. "I'm the only one who can do this."

"Believe it. Own it. Let it drive you." Her words rang with the force of command. "Let it course through your veins."

"I will." My voice echoed her conviction.

"Let justice rain down on all the evildoers of this world." With her cry, she threw her arms open in a triumphant gesture.

Following her lead, I raised my arms, too, though what I really wanted was for her to hug me like she'd done when I was a child. But those days had long gone.

"Let me just finish locking this stuff up." I reached for the door handle. "Can you stay? Please, stay. We'll celebrate and make plans."

When I looked back, she had vanished, leaving the air empty and cold where moments ago warmth and assurance had resided. My heart sank.

My mother, my guardian angel, came only when I needed

her most. And she stayed just long enough to remind me how much I missed her.

I crumpled into my emotions, counting to ten, then brought them to a full stop. Once I was composed, I straightened, brushed off my knees, and got back to work. The inside of the safe gleamed black by the time I finished, more than a dozen handguns lining its shelves. I had a cache of ammunition plentiful enough to last me until the end of days, stacked and ready to load.

There were maps too. Homes and neighborhoods with multiple entrances and exits marked. Traffic patterns. Work schedules. Names and descriptions of friends, family, and coworkers who were most likely to come and go. Everything had been downloaded and printed from libraries and public access computers that were miles apart to dilute any digital fingerprints and confuse any trail left in my wake.

I stood, hands on my hips, admiring my accomplishment. I couldn't keep all of the handguns, of course. Taking them only served to throw the cops off my scent. If I got caught with this many stolen firearms—now or later—that would ruin all my plans. So I'd sell what I didn't need and keep enough guns to finish my mission. Switching weapons with every kill would further muddle my tracks.

The plan was foolproof, and my work was superb.

She should have seen this. Should have stayed all the way through to the end. But that was how it was with my mother. She never stuck around, always gone far too soon.

9

After their chat with Bryce Faulkner, Lucas got a call to head to the office of the medical examiner. The postmortem exam was complete, and Dr. Simon wanted to update the agents on his findings.

The landscape rushed by Lucas's passenger-side window. Patches of early spring weeds were punctuated by small piles of litter accumulated over the long winter. A sad reminder of humanity's disrespect for the land, but it was preferable to the memories threatening to break through Lucas's mental barricades.

He'd known returning to the Violent Crime Unit would reawaken ghosts he wasn't prepared to confront.

But at that moment, all Lucas could picture was Sam Faulkner's body on a sterile table, cold and gray.

"You okay over there?" Journey glanced at him from behind the wheel. "We haven't worked together long enough for me to read your silence."

"Just focused, is all." Lucas didn't want to reveal what was cluttering up his thoughts.

To Journey's credit, she gave him about a mile before

piping up again. "Anything you want to share? I can do maybe a half hour in silence, but the full hour back to Pittsburgh might make me worry you don't love me anymore." She shot him a grin.

"Not a fan of pathology visits," Lucas confessed.

"Ah." From her tone, she wasn't surprised.

They wouldn't see the body. The exam was already done. But all the triggers would be there. The hints of refrigerated steel tainted with iron-rich blood. Chemically sanitized instruments. Bleached floors. Smell was a powerful memory trigger.

He pushed his fist hard against his lips, choking back vomit.

"Whoa." Journey slowed the car. "Need me to pull over?"

Lucas shook his head. "I'm fine. Just keep driving."

"Copy that." The accelerator purred in response.

After a few more miles of silence, Journey glanced over at him again. "Just so you know, I'm fighting my every instinct to give you a lot of shit right now."

"Can't say I'd be as disciplined as you if the roles were reversed."

"Points for me, then." She shot him a side-eye. Probably evaluating the shades of green on his face.

He couldn't blame her. The intensity of his reaction surprised him too. "I'm not usually this weak-stomached."

"Not sure anyone ever gets used to seeing the pathologist's knife slice open a human body."

"Ugh." That nearly did it. "You intentionally torturing me?"

"Sorry. Couldn't help myself." She pressed harder on the accelerator. "But look, if you're talking, you're not puking. So how 'bout you try that for a while?"

At this point, he'd try anything. "Reminds me of one of my first cases."

"That bad, huh?"

"Forced me out of Violent Crimes for twelve years."

She gripped the steering wheel tight, turning her knuckles white. "Sometimes the stuff we witness hits a little too close to home."

"You can say that again." Another wave of nausea rolled through Lucas. He breathed slowly, letting it pass. "The boyfriend of one of the crime scene techs in the Alaska field office snapped. Turned a domestic into an hours-long standoff with law enforcement."

"Horrible," Journey murmured.

"Had a gun pressed to her head while her twelve-year-old daughter watched. He kept screaming that if we were so good, how come we were powerless to stop him from killing them all?"

Lucas dropped his forehead to the window, aching for cool as heat rushed his body. His legs trembled, and he was glad he wasn't driving.

Journey flipped on the blinker and eased onto the exit ramp. "I've been there. That's the battle, isn't it? Constantly having to reconcile just how little power we have."

Lucas pushed the weak air out of his lungs, trying to inhale a calming breath. "He shot her and her daughter in front of everyone. Like he wanted an audience."

It was sick. Evil, maybe. An image Lucas had tried to keep at bay for more than a decade. For a lifetime, more like. What was he doing, returning to VC?

I'm not ready.

"My dad killed my mom the same way. Shot her in the head in a drunken rage."

Journey pulled over. She put the car in park but kept the engine running. "Oh man, I'm sorry. I didn't know."

He shook his head, gritting his teeth as he waved her back onto the road. "I'm alive. At least I've got that."

She gave him one last look before pulling back into traffic like he'd asked. "I've got your back in there. Just give me a signal, and I'll make an excuse for you to go get some fresh air."

Lucas appreciated her offer more than he could say.

Dr. Smith Simon met with them in his office a little over an hour later. Medical tomes teetered in stacks on his desk, in his chair, and along bookshelves threatening collapse. The man himself reminded Lucas of a mad scientist in his long, white lab coat with a puff of crazy white hair to match.

Despite Lucas's amusing mental image of Dr. Simon cackling over bubbling glass cylinders, his palms sweated as he and Journey stood in the cold, sterile, neutral, featureless beige and steel of the medical examiner's office, listening to the forensic pathology report. He breathed in through his nose and out through his mouth to quell the cramps clawing at his stomach.

Dr. Simon's findings were expected. Sam Faulkner had suffered a single gunshot wound to the abdomen that tore through his stomach and upper intestines. The fatal blow came from the blunt force trauma, fracturing the skull and causing an epidural hematoma. Body temperature and signs of early stage rigor mortis at the scene led Dr. Simon to estimate the time of death somewhere between four and seven in the evening.

Journey flipped through her notes. "Sam pulled the day's sales data from the POS system at five eighteen. PBP got the shots-fired call around six. So the timelines add up."

The forensic pathologist crossed his arms. "Other than that, though, I suspect there's nothing groundbreaking for you in my report."

"What about the DNA results from the flakes of blood?" Journey held up both hands, fingers crossed.

Dr. Simon's gray eyebrows drew down over his nose like an amassing thundercloud. "I'm still waiting for the park ranger's results to be loaded into the system so I'll have something to match too."

"How about a tox screen?" Crime scene investigators had already reported they found no indication of substances in the tumbler of bourbon, but Lucas liked to exclude any possibilities as firmly as possible.

"Not back yet, but I'll let you know if we find anything."

After thanking him for his time, they made their way out of the ACOME offices. Journey checked her watch. "How is it already almost three o'clock? I'm famished. Think you can stomach food yet?"

Lucas shook his head. "How 'bout you grab a sandwich while I get the car? I'll drive, you eat."

"Deal."

He picked her up from the deli around the corner, and as she slid into the passenger seat, Journey handed him a sandwich. "I took a chance. Plain old turkey on wheat. In case you get hungry later." She winked. "Coffee and sandwiches for everyone. You know...in the spirit of starting this partnership off right."

Lucas expected he'd end up stashing it in the staff refrigerator for later, but he appreciated her gesture.

At the field office, they headed to the second-floor forensic unit. Lucas wasn't a superstitious man, but he crossed his fingers as they walked down the hallway. They needed a break, some new piece of evidence to point the way toward a suspect. The M.E. hadn't provided it, but maybe forensics would.

Rae Peterson was the tech assigned to their case. Lucas found her station and barely had time to introduce Journey and himself before she launched into her findings.

"As you know, two casings were recovered. One three-eighty ACP, one nine millimeter. The nine millimeter was consistent with the weapon found on scene." She tucked a strand of her blond pixie behind her ear. "Analysis on the three-eighty showed rifling consistent with Browning Black Label nineteen-eleven three-eighty."

Lucas hadn't worked with her before, but he liked that she spoke in bullet points. Easy to follow without the fluff. Much like the plain, black t-shirt and jeans she wore beneath her lab coat. She might've been five feet nothing, but her confidence made up for her small stature.

"The on-scene weapon was a Glock nineteen registered in Faulkner's name," Journey read from her notebook. "It was found a few feet from Sam's body."

"Judging from the directionality of the hole in the wall and the nine-millimeter bullet retrieved from it," Rae gestured as if holding an imaginary gun in each hand, "your guy got a single shot off at his attacker but missed."

Nothing in Rae's report so far contradicted their early suspicions.

"The bullet from the recovered three-eighty casing," Rae continued, "was removed from the victim's body during the autopsy."

Journey flipped through her notebook pages. "And I assume you matched rifling on the bullet to the same Browning?"

"We did." Rae turned to her computer and clicked a few tabs, bringing up photographs. "Side-by-side evidence photos of the casings found at the scene, tagged and numbered as evidence."

"Appears both Faulkner and his attacker got off a single shot, though only one of them hit its mark." Lucas winced. If he were attacked, he'd like to imagine he wouldn't have missed. "Which would be odd, given Sam's line of work. I'd expect him to be a decent marksman."

Journey nodded. "The perp took him by surprise."

"Speaking of." Lucas tapped his skull. "How about the trauma to the head?"

Rae clicked another tab on her computer and brought up the photograph of what looked like grains of sand. "We tested the debris around the body and found quartzite mineral deposits. No rocks large enough to have caused the victim's head trauma were found around the crime scene."

"So our perp brought a rock from home?"

"Or from his last kill." Rae pulled up the file on the park ranger. "Quartzite mineral deposits were also found on the body of Noah Hudson, so the perp very well might have picked a rock up at that national park where he was killed."

Journey moved closer to the monitor. "So our perp took a souvenir from his first kill and used it to finish off Faulkner?"

"The mineral type would be consistent with the kinds of rock found in the area where Noah Hudson was murdered. And the flakes of blood add weight to that theory too."

"Okay. How about fingerprints?" Journey bent over Rae's shoulder as she pulled Faulkner's file back up on screen.

"No." Rae shook her head. "But we examined the footprints found at the scene. One bloody footprint discovered near Sam's body belonged to someone wearing a men's size twelve."

Journey arched her eyebrow. "You said footprints? Plural?"

"Yes." Rae nodded. "A second matching and even clearer footprint was found in the dirt in the alley behind the gun shop. Same size, same tread."

"With those two matching footprints, we have confirmation that our perp entered from the alley." Journey smiled. "Two steps forward—"

Lucas held up a palm, bringing out a frown from Journey. "Sure, but we still don't have any suspects." The pieces were there, but like a puzzle without a reference photo, Lucas didn't know how to put them together.

It was time to take their findings to the whiteboard.

10

Tuesday morning, after cordoning off the wall by their desks the previous evening, Journey and Lucas were still working on the murder board. They'd placed Sam Faulkner and his shop in the top center, along with the size twelve footprints and missing semiautomatic pistols. Bryce Faulkner and The Chosen branched off to the left. The right side listed Noah Hudson, the park ranger from West Virginia. Connecting them was the gut shot, cranial blunt trauma, and quartzite mineral deposits.

In a corner, the foreign blood type featured a big question mark. They couldn't conclude that possible connection until the blood flake found on Sam Faulkner came back as a match for Noah Hudson.

But even with all that, the board remained largely empty.

They'd agreed to go their separate ways at nearly nine last night. Journey had hoped a good night of sleep would bring clarity to the board in front of her this morning.

It hadn't. Not even when Lucas arrived with a jumbo-sized coffee.

She stood back and examined what they had.

"All signs for Sam Faulkner's murder point to theft." Journey crossed her arms and drummed her fingers against her bicep. "Bryce Faulkner is connected to Sam, but how do the Faulkner brothers connect with Noah Hudson? It can't be simply about stealing because nothing was stolen from Hudson. They're similar in the manner they were both killed, but even the same weapon wasn't used."

While Sam Faulkner had died by a Browning 1911, Noah Hudson was killed with a hunting rifle, a Marlin 336.

Journey wrinkled her nose in distaste at her next thought. "And we can't ignore Bryce's connection to The Chosen, can we?"

"It's too early to eliminate The Righties as a possibility," Lucas agreed. "But we have to follow the evidence."

There were numerous groups with incentive to kill a gun shop owner. Pittsburgh weathered the existence of many criminal organizations within its borders, everything from the Mafia to drug cartels and human trafficking rings. They all needed firearms, and none were above killing to get them.

Overnight, ATF Agent Dubovsky had sent over the final inventory of thirteen missing weapons and six hundred rounds of ammunition, with the serial numbers of every firearm flagged. If any of the stolen guns turned up in a future crime, they'd immediately notify all agencies. This was a small comfort, given that a crime had to occur to get Sam's firearms off the streets. But at least it was something.

"We need to dig deeper." Journey's brain itched to fill in some gaps. "You said you've got a pal in Cyber."

Lucas nodded. "I played softball with a few of the analysts."

She didn't know they even had a team, but that was a question for another day. "Think they've had time to review Sam's security system or any of his neighbors' surveillance footage?"

"Only one way to find out." Lucas motioned for Journey to follow him. They took the stairs down to the third floor, where the Cyber Crimes and Intelligence Analysis teams worked.

The hum of activity on the third floor was exhilarating.

Journey glanced around, taking in the intense activity and cacophony of noise as agents in business casual huddled around their computer monitors—scrolling through images, talking on phones, and feverishly typing reports. Three flat-screen monitors lined up behind each workstation, creating an almost robotic aura.

It made her proud to work within a system of people so dedicated to their jobs.

Lucas marched right up to a tall man with shoulders like an ox and clapped him on his shoulder. "Hey, Tim."

"So this is the shortstop of the field office softball team?" Journey held her hand out. "Nice to meet another one of Agent Sullivan's friends."

"Tim Cranz." He grasped Journey's hand in a powerful grip.

"Sorry." Lucas smacked himself on the forehead. "This is my partner, Special Agent Journey Russo."

"You come down here to show off, or do you need something from me?" Cranz threw a faux punch at Lucas's arm.

"A little of both." Lucas nodded toward Cranz's monitors. "You got anything from the security cameras at Faulkner's on Sunday?"

"Yeah. I was just going over those." Cranz sat down at his workstation, where he had multiple monitors running. As his fingers flew across the keys, video windows popped up on the screens. "Faulkner's Guns and Ammo wasn't located in a particularly busy neighborhood. But the cameras in the back alley picked up some activity."

Cranz took Journey and Lucas through the highlights of the footage from the window of time leading up to Sam's murder.

"The Greek restaurant next door saw about a dozen customers come and go. The coffee shop across the street caught the employee who closed up for the night walking to their car in the parking lot. Cameras at the gun shop cut out just before six."

"That wasn't long before Faulkner's approximate time of death." Journey pulled her notebook from her back pocket and flipped it open. "Which the M.E. had pegged sometime before six." It helped to narrow the window considerably. Sam Faulkner had made an entry in the POS system at a quarter past five, which meant they were looking at a time frame of around forty-five minutes.

"Prior to the cameras going dark, there was nothing out of the ordinary," Cranz continued. "Employees clock out and leave around four, then Sam brings his work out to the front counter and stays there. Focuses on his tasks. No indication he hears anything, never startles. Then, like I said, it cuts out."

Pittsburgh Bureau of Police—their team was first on scene Sunday night—were conducting initial interviews with Faulkner's employees, starting with the ones who'd worked at the shop the day of the murder. Journey had checked in with them earlier in the morning and learned that all the staff members had expressed the same grief and surprise over Sam's murder. All had alibis. None wore size-twelve shoes.

Apparently, he'd been a great boss, run a tight ship, followed all the laws carefully, and treated people with respect. According to staff at Faulkner's Guns & Ammo, nothing concerning appeared to have occurred on Sunday or any day.

Journey leaned in toward the screen. "Anything of interest with the footage from the neighboring businesses?"

"There is this." Cranz clicked on a file, and another video window appeared on his screen. "The copy and print shop farther down the strip maintains a second camera above its rear alley entrance. Mostly footage of an employee going out for smoke breaks. But it recorded a lone figure hurrying toward the gun shop at 5:47 p.m."

He hit play, and he and Lucas joined Journey in leaning forward with anticipation. The clip was only twenty seconds long, so they watched it several times through.

The footage, while intriguing, wasn't the Holy Grail. It was grainy and dark but clear enough to determine that the unsub was male, likely white or possibly Hispanic. As the person of interest passed the camera, he crossed by a *No Parking* sign that provided enough of a height reference to place him around five-ten. Unfortunately, he'd pulled a neck gator across the bottom half of his face. He also seemed to know exactly when to turn away from the camera.

Did he case the place?

Journey pushed her chair back from the screen and relaxed her shoulders. "It's interesting, but what does it tell us?"

Cranz let out a sheepish sigh. "Not as much as I'd wanted."

"That guy looks too short to be the owner of a size-twelve shoe print." Lucas lifted his foot for comparison. "I'm taller than him, and I wear eleven and a half."

Burly Cranz pulled up his pant leg. "Thirteen."

"Foot size and height aren't equal indicators. I knew a guy no bigger than me who wore size-twelve shoes." Journey flipped through the pages of her notebook. "Faulkner was five eleven and had a shoe size of...twelve."

The three of them turned back to the grainy image of the masked man on the screen.

Journey tapped her pen against her book. "We know that can't be Sam, though, correct? Security footage shows him inside when this is recorded?"

"Yes." Cranz leaned in closer to the screen. "And whether Faulkner expects it or not, he's about to get a visitor. Question is, is it this guy?"

11

Norman Perry straightened the strangling knot of his navy blue necktie with frustration as he strode up the walkway to his front door.

It was only Tuesday night, but he'd already hit his limit of bullshit for the week.

He didn't know how he was going to make it through to Friday without losing it on someone. Everyone at the office had developed a case of stupid. He'd talked his throat raw, trying to explain simple concepts, but his staff just seemed to get dumber by the minute.

Except for Karen, his assistant. She was just hypercritical and hyper-focused by nature.

"Mr. Perry, did you know you have a spot on your shirt?" Norman mocked her high-pitched tone.

He growled low in his throat. "This is a custom-tailored, navy blue suit...and all she noticed was one microscopic speck of coffee. No comment about the fresh shine on my loafers or the precision trim of my sideburns."

Norman pushed the key in the door and twisted.

"All she can do is criticize me. And just to rub salt in the wound, she put a reminder on my calendar to tell the dry cleaner when I drop it off. Like I'm incompetent. The nerve of that woman."

Coming home to an empty house didn't help Norman's sour mood. His ex-wife might've been a nag, but when she was around, at least the house had been warm and smelled like heaven. Rigatoni. Baked chicken. If he was really lucky…steak.

God, what he wouldn't give for one more bowl of her Yankee pot roast.

Only, Barbara was three hundred miles away, probably making dinner for Roger What's His Face.

The kids were the ones to drop that bomb but refused to tell Norman more than the guy's name. Like they were lording prized information over him.

Let her date. I only missed her cooking anyway.

Honestly, he was better off not knowing anything. Their relationship was over. She wanted to move on, so Norman showed her the door.

Bye-bye, Barbara.

His son, Jack, had better things to focus on than who his mom was dating this week.

From what Norman had seen, the boy was struggling to get through his coursework at UVA. If his GPA dropped below a 3.5, he'd lose his scholarship.

As for Gina, his daughter…Norman just hoped she wasn't using "divorce trauma" as a case study for her psychology thesis. Arizona State had a reputation for hard partying, but Gina was too type A to let distractions get in the way of her academic goals. At least with her, Norman might recoup his investment. The way his life was going, he'd need a therapist before too long.

The door hinges screamed for oil as he shoved his way into the house. Sure enough, the only scent coming from the kitchen was disappointment. Nothing baking in there except the garbage he'd neglected to take out before work that morning.

Norman cursed himself, yanking the bag out of the bin and knotting it as he headed for the garage. He opened the door and slammed his fist against the light switch as he crossed the threshold.

It remained stubbornly dark, mocking him. With a roar of rage, he flipped the switch again.

On. Off. On. Off.

Nothing.

"Dammit!" Temper rising, he spun around a bit too fast, stumbled blindly, and slammed his knee into…something.

"Son of a…" This day needed to end. The sooner, the better.

Squinting in pain, he noticed the lights in the rest of the house had also gone off.

"Just can't catch a break, can I?" Norman hobbled back inside, leaving the trash bag on the garage floor. It joined the large pile of boxes and bags that had taken up residence in the large space. It was so junked up, he had to park in the damn driveway.

The electrician he'd had out last month was going to get an earful in tomorrow's voicemail.

For now, he'd have to fix things himself. As usual. At this rate, he'd have to change out an entire box of fuses.

Grabbing a flashlight, he started downstairs to the basement.

A shuffling below stopped him midway. The movement was way too pronounced to have come from a small critter. Not a mouse or rat. Raccoon, maybe?

Boxes tipped over, spilling what sounded like old pots and pans on the cement floor.

"Hello?" If someone was down there, he was going to give

them one chance to change their mind. "I'm armed, and you're trespassing on my property. In the eyes of the law, I don't have to justify shooting you."

Carefully, he backed up the stairs to his kitchen, rushed to the knife rack, and grabbed the biggest blade he could find.

His guns were too far away to be of much use. He hadn't been hunting in years, so he'd stashed them in a gun locker upstairs.

Since this whole "noise in the basement" was probably just a harmless varmint or his exhaustion and frustration at the end of a long day playing tricks on him, he wasn't about to take the time to go get them. The chances someone was lying in wait for him downstairs were next to zero. Of course, maybe it was likely enough to scare them back out the way they'd come in.

He added *Fix that outer lock* to the never-ending list of repairs in his head. The house was old. Maybe it was all in his imagination. The noise might have just been the furnace giving out. That was more like the kind of luck he had. And if that was the case, he'd better get down there and look at it.

Wouldn't that be the perfect way to end his monumentally shitty day…freezing to death?

Butcher knife in hand, Norman descended to the basement again. This time, he sidestepped the creaking steps and waited to click on his flashlight beam until he reached the bottom. The cold, damp air of the basement floor swallowed him with each step he took. The pressing darkness seemed almost alive.

He saw nothing but black…right up until a figure lunged from the shadows. The flashlight flew from Norman's grip as his reflexes worked a split second too late. His blade made contact, though, eliciting a muted hiss of pain, confirming Norman's strike had done damage.

"I warned you, you son of a bitch!" Norman shouted before something like a freight train crashed into him.

Fire exploded in his belly as he registered the lightning-quick strike of a bullet tearing into his abdomen. He was mid-fall by the time a cry of agony left his lips. His ass hit concrete, sending another arc of pain straight up his tailbone.

Norman tilted to the side and crumpled as he felt for the fire in his belly. His fingers found a warm wetness.

A mocking voice called out from the darkness. "Well, well…"

Norman attempted to stem the flow of blood running down his stomach while frantically searching for his knife on the slick ground.

His fallen flashlight cast eerie, fleeting shadows across the walls and floor. Norman spotted his knife, but it was nowhere within reach.

"You went down even faster than your friend." The disembodied voice apparently came from all around him, even though that couldn't be possible.

He had to be close, though.

Norman's vision constricted to pinholes of light as he searched for his attacker. "Why…?"

"What a disappointment. I'd hoped to watch you suffer. Pictured it in my mind. But the fantasy was so much more satisfying than this. You're just a worthless old man on a concrete floor with no idea what he's even dying for."

Norman tried to make sense of the words. His life hadn't been worthless.

"What do you—"

A heavy object struck him on the side of the head. His vision exploded into a thousand stars and extinguished, sending Norman into oblivion.

12

Two men crossed off my list. Three, if I chose to count the practice shot I'd taken with that ranger. Either way, they all went off without so much as a hiccup in their execution.

I pocketed the rock I'd used to bash in Norman Perry's skull and leaned over to pick up the knife Perry had naively believed would protect him. Killing him hadn't been the satisfying scene of justice I'd built up in my imagination.

Then again, it was my fault for making him a more worthy adversary in my mind. Even Faulkner with all his guns went down with hardly any effort. In reality, those men were just pudgy, middle-aged weaklings.

Maybe that was just how it was supposed to go. Wicked men, like Faulkner and Perry, were meant to go down with a whimper rather than with a blaze of glory.

I stood there, knife in hand, contemplating my next move as the blood leaked out of Perry's lifeless body. It had been too easy, too simple. Still, I couldn't deny the rush of adrenaline that coursed through my veins as I watched the light leave his eyes. That rush was stronger than anything else I could ever remember feeling.

What would Mother think now? She always said I was meant for greatness.

I clenched the knife, its handle digging into my palms.

Is this greatness? Am I the hand of divine justice?

With that part of the plan completed, I rushed up the stairs to rummage for cash or valuables, leaving cupboard doors and drawers open as I ransacked. I had to make sure it looked like a robbery. No one could know about my list, least of all the police. Law enforcement needed to think the robberies were unconnected. The world, however, would see these corrupt men brought to justice.

As I rummaged through the pantry, an old coffee can caught my attention. With five hundred dollars tucked inside, I couldn't resist. But my fingers quivered as I grabbed the cash, feeling a pang of guilt at taking money that wasn't mine.

Judging from Norman's half-acre lawn and the BMW in the driveway, I'd have thought he'd have more goodies to choose from. *His wife must have picked him clean in the divorce.*

Norman wouldn't need that money any longer, so I snagged it and moved on to the bedroom, snatching a gold wedding band and watch from the dresser.

Pockets bulging, I headed back downstairs. My heart raced faster as I savored how close I was to completing tonight's mission.

With all I had come for in hand, I made it to the kitchen sink to take care of any DNA evidence. Carefully and methodically, I scrubbed the knife with bleach and warm water until there was nothing left but a pristine surface.

Then I pulled a bandana from my pocket and polished the gun, making sure no prints remained. After running downstairs and wiping away every last trace of evidence, I went back to the main floor, tucked both weapons in my pocket, and made for the door.

My mother's presence lingered as if she were watching me proudly from above. I'd brought justice to those who deserved it, and the police would never be able to trace the deaths back to me.

But still...there was something missing. I needed to see my mother's smile in person. Hopefully, when I returned home, she'd be there to congratulate me on a job well done.

I stepped outside into the night. The cooling breeze blowing against my skin felt like a blessing for all I had accomplished this evening.

Just to cover my bases, I circled the block, looking for a good place to dispose of the weapons. Like a sign from the gods that my mission was righteous, a construction dumpster had been left unlocked. The perfect place to get rid of any evidence.

After a quick glance around to make sure nobody was watching, I tossed the knife and gun inside and observed as they disappeared into the debris. The only thing I kept was the rock. It still had work to do.

Then, calm and collected, I crept away, disappearing into the gloom.

13

By Wednesday afternoon, Journey was actively fighting her frustration with their investigation.

Sure, they'd gotten a silhouette of a possible perp from the alley camera. A male of unknown racial descent and average height and weight with no distinguishing features, dressed in plain, solid-colored clothing.

A lot of good that did.

"The latest update from Cyber concludes that a virus shut down Faulkner's entire system. That was why the automated backup generator in the store failed when the power was cut." Lucas scanned down the page he'd just pulled off the printer. "They have yet to determine the specifics on how the virus was uploaded into the system, but it's likely the perp accessed the server directly with a flash drive."

"How is that an update?" Journey didn't know the first thing about the inner workings of a computer and hadn't meant to disparage the work of Cyber. But in her need to vent her frustration, an absent target was an easy mark.

"Should I read the rest or just pin it on the board?" Lucas

was getting a little testy as well. Investigating for three days with nothing to show was making them both cranky.

"Sorry. Go ahead. Did they say anything about the door?"

After Lucas returned to the page, his eyebrows arched in a curious expression. "The alarm at the door appears to have been remotely disarmed by a replay attack."

"What's a replay attack?"

He gave her a crooked smile. "Well, I'm glad you asked. According to our expert…" Lucas cleared his throat like he was the mayor about to give a speech, then read from the report. "'The data logs before Faulkner's system shut down showed no unauthorized entry. A beam-steerable, phased-array antenna, with a standard range of six hundred feet, is a device capable of capturing signals from remote key fobs and or radio frequency identification cards. It can also repeat those stolen signals. A perpetrator using such a device could easily disarm the door and camera movement sensor as they came down the alley without creating an alert.'"

"Whoever this perp is, they must have some impressive tech skills." Journey mimed clicking a remote. "*Boop*. Disarmed. Then just stroll right on in like you own the place."

"Sam Faulkner didn't even know what was coming." Lucas set the paper down on his desk with a sigh.

"We need a new angle of attack," she waved her hand at the board, "if we hope to identify this guy."

"You said that yesterday." Lucas began to pace. As he walked, he played with the strap on his watch. She'd seen him do that a few times. It was his tell. Lucas didn't like not having answers. But he wasn't giving up. And neither was she.

"And I'll keep saying it until we figure out what we're missing. There's got to be something in the evidence we've collected that can help us identify this guy."

"What about...no." Lucas shook his head and mumbled something. His pacing radius grew with each lap he took.

Journey focused on the board, desperate to fill out the section that read, *Victim Profile*. "C'mon. Take it step-by-step. What do we know about our victims?"

She considered the lonely picture of the park ranger, Noah Hudson. He was an outdoorsy guy right from the start. Worked his way up to Eagle Scout before heading off to college. Got his bachelor's in forest resources management from WVU. Interned with student conservation associations.

His record was spotless. He'd been working alone to prep a campsite for opening season. He lived and worked in the Monongahela National Park. No wife, no ex-wives, no children, nothing to suggest he had any enemies.

She lifted an eyebrow. "Why would anyone want to hurt him?"

"And why would anyone want to hurt him *and* Sam Faulkner? What's the connection?"

Noah Hudson was a mystery that offered few clues. Everything about his background was so straightforward. The man had lived and breathed the forest.

Journey turned to the other side of the board. Faulkner, however, at least had some strings worth pulling on.

"Okay, Faulkner. What was going on with your gun store and the people who frequented it?"

PBP Detective Patty Traynor had completed her interviews with Faulkner's employees and found nothing of note. It was a small shop, just four team members besides Sam. Each of them professed admiration for their former boss, and they also had confirmed alibis for Sunday evening. Two were attending a mutual friend's birthday dinner. One was at his weekly Bible study, and the other was in the hospital, recovering from gallbladder surgery.

"Maybe not a current employee. Who else had access to

the shop?" Journey's focus moved to the list of peripheral connections to the gun shop. No one else held the keys or code to Faulkner's security system. He had a policy procedure for everything and everybody who came into his business.

The system recognized one key fob for keyless entry. That was on Sam Faulkner's keys. Anyone other than him who arrived at the back door would trigger the security camera. The system was app-enabled and attached to his phone, so when he was away from the shop, he'd get a ping if anyone or anything triggered the camera at the door. If he didn't approve them, they couldn't get through.

"Except for the one who did." Journey reached up to the pendant hanging from her neck and rubbed the gold ace of diamonds charm. She needed a little good luck right about now. "Who are you?"

As Lucas lapped the office, Journey continued talking to herself. "Everyone was vetted, and Faulkner knew each of them by name." Faulkner had done background checks on every member of his team and all the people, including the weekly cleaning crew, who serviced the gun store.

"This feels like an inside job." When Lucas stopped beside her, he looked like he was trying to convince himself more than anything.

"I know. That's what I keep coming back to. Faulkner was a stickler for doing things by the book. Everyone who came into the store was triple-checked." Still rubbing her necklace charm, she took a step closer to their board, hoping something would stand out. Some detail they hadn't spotted. "And yet, I keep coming back to the door. No sign of forced entry. They had to know what kind of security Faulkner had, right?"

"Not necessarily. If the perp had the technical know-how,

he might not need to know the specific system." Lucas stepped forward as well.

"So we're dealing with someone who's been lying in wait for their opportunity to get Faulkner, or a highly capable hacker." She scoffed. "That narrows things down."

"You're forgetting the third option." Lucas pressed his fingers like he was rubbing two coins together. "Someone with the money to pay for the necessary tech skills."

Journey hadn't investigated many high-tech cases during her career, but she should've considered hacking for hire. "Which begs the question of motive. Why did they break in and kill Faulkner?" Journey double-checked the numbers the ATF had given for the stolen guns. "Were thirteen guns and six hundred rounds of ammunition really worth cracking Sam's security for? Or were the guns a misdirection?"

It didn't add up. This was looking less like a simple burglary.

"I see where your head is." Lucas waggled a finger at her as he slid into his seat. "We need to dig a little deeper into Faulkner's financials. See if he got himself into any money trouble. Something he had to keep quiet to avoid ruining his reputation."

"It's like we're sharing one mind right now." Journey took her seat and searched for the number Tammie Faulkner had given her for Sam's accountant. "Significant debt could be an indication he'd been forced to borrow money from less-than-legal entities."

"Maybe he had to reach out to powerful families with dubious morals and more than enough resources to spend in eliminating Sam if he turned out to be a bad debt."

"Exactly. We need to look for signs of," Journey air-quoted, "'creative accounting.' And keep an eye out for Noah Hudson's name. Maybe they had some kind of financial arrangement or shared a passion for firearms."

Cursory glances into Faulkner's background hadn't raised flags about financial or legal trouble, but Journey turned her eye on his accounts with a special focus on unusual amounts of assets being sold or moved between them.

Hours later, she leaned back with a small smile, then stood and cracked her aching neck. "Sam Faulkner is one of the most type A businesspeople I've ever investigated."

Lucas laughed so hard, he snorted. "He doesn't just file his documents alphabetically. He subcategorizes them by date, region, and..." he shuffled a file in front of him, "even paper color, from what I can tell."

They hadn't uncovered a single statement of noncompliance with state firearms regulations. Taxes were filed on time. He was even up to date on his payroll.

"However..." Journey let her voice trail off, drawing Lucas's attention. "I found this." She picked up a file she'd been populating with pages during her search. "Some odd receipts for a hunting trip Sam Faulkner took in West Virginia."

"Nothing odd about a hunting trip with the boys." Lucas casually glanced toward the murder board, then back at Journey. Then she watched the thought click in his head as he faced her.

"West Virginia, you say?"

"Yep. They went to—"

"Monongahela?" He'd cut her off with a small smile.

"Bingo."

He pointed to Noah Hudson's picture on the murder board. "The park ranger—"

"That's where he works...worked." She'd cut him off this time. "I still need to cross-check the dates with his employment history. Sam's hunting trip was about seven years ago."

"Wow. He kept receipts for a hunting trip from seven

years ago?"

Journey shrugged. "You've seen his paperwork. The man should've worked for the IRS."

"Okay. Are you going to make me guess what happened or torture me with small nuggets of information?"

"I found a National Park Service case file that came up about that same time." Journey chewed on her lower lip, relishing this moment of tension. "I don't want to get my hopes up, but it's sounding like we found ourselves a connecting point."

"I'm dying of old age here." Lucas rolled his eyes and held out his hand. "Either give me the file or the details but don't keep me waiting for answers."

"Okay. Here it is. Sam Faulkner and a few of his buddies were out hunting near the Monongahela. We have receipts for hunting licenses. Cabin rental. Miscellaneous food. The accounting looked normal up to that point." She paused for dramatic effect. "Then I saw some receipts for rifles and ammunition. He'd purchased enough to cover the hunting trip."

"Sounds like Faulkner was using the business account for personal purchases." Lucas raised a skeptical eyebrow. "Who hasn't done that?"

"*He* doesn't do that." Journey shook her head in disbelief.

"Maybe he does, and he's just better at it than most. How does this connect to the case you found?" Impatience rang in Lucas's tone.

"Based on what I saw in his ledgers, he claimed he was testing new equipment before stocking it in his store. But we can't really alert the IRS about that now, can we?" Journey chuckled as she flipped through her notes.

Lucas cleared his throat in a very *hurry up* way, adding a wrist roll in case she didn't catch on.

"Okay…here's where it gets interesting." Journey picked

up the reports she'd received from the National Park Service. Any case or incident Noah Hudson had signed or been listed on was summarized in the files. She pointed at one of the notes from seven years ago. "I've submitted a request for the full case file, but this is what I managed to pull up. One of the men on the hunting trip, Jerry Minton, was killed."

Lucas frowned. "Can't they just email it to us?"

Journey blew out a long breath. "They had a server go down a couple years back, so they're having to dig through physical files, then scan them in before sending."

"Hope they do that quick." Lucas leaned forward in his chair and rested his elbows on his knees. "I'm guessing Jerry took a bullet meant for a buck?"

"Unfortunately...yes."

"Bet Sam Faulkner chose not to stock that particular rifle in his store."

Journey snorted. "Oh, he still stocked the rifle."

"Ever the businessman." Lucas nodded. "Was anyone charged for Jerry Minton's death?"

"There were no charges." She scanned the report. "They ruled the incident an accident."

"Any creative accounting around that time period?" Lucas met Journey's gaze again.

"If you were thinking about bribery...no." She shook her head. "I was looking for that. The only accounting mistake I saw was the earlier one I mentioned. And...that's pretty much where things stop."

"Seven years ago, you say?" Lucas scrubbed a hand over his face.

"Yeah. I know it's been a long time since that hunting trip. I'm sure we're well past the statute of limitations on involuntary manslaughter too."

His brow furrowed. "But you're thinking that trip has something to do with what's happening now?"

"I can't say for certain." Journey shrugged even as her mind churned over the possibilities. "And I don't want to jump to any conclusions. But we can't deny the potential connection between Sam and Noah."

"It's definitely something worth checking into." Lucas nodded. "But—"

"Look." Journey cut him off before he could say anything she didn't want to hear. "I've been hunting for accounting issues for hours and can't find a single purchase that isn't cross-referenced in triplicate with receipts to back it up. My *bad debt with the mob* theory is looking pretty weak at this point."

"So the trip's all we got?"

Journey slid the file across the desk to Lucas. "This hunting trip connection, old as it is, might at least lead us to a better clue." She wasn't sure what they would uncover, but at this point, she'd do just about anything if it'd save her from having to read one more of Sam Faulkner's cash flow statements. Hell, she'd interview the family pet if it got her out of the office.

Lucas thumbed through the pages before setting the file back on the desk. "You know this means going back to a mourning widow and asking her about the *other time* her husband was involved in a shooting."

"That's the job. Sniffing out every potential lead." Journey let out a long, tired breath. "Tammie Faulkner's going to be so happy to see us again."

14

Tammie Faulkner wore a wary smile as she opened the door of her suburban home. "Afternoon, Agent Russo, Agent Sullivan. Do you have news for me?"

"Not yet." Journey tried to look sympathetic as she met Tammie's intense gaze. She wished she had a way of sounding more optimistic. Tammie was mourning the loss of her husband, and rather than coming to tell the grieving widow news that they'd found the murderer, she and her partner were there to probe into Sam Faulkner's history. "We're following up on some leads and were hoping you might help us with a little background information."

"I don't know what else I can tell you about Sam, but if it helps find his murderer, okay." Tammie nodded, her face solemn. She motioned for the agents to sit down in the living room.

Journey and Lucas stepped inside and settled on the couch.

"First," Lucas cleared his throat, "I have to say, your husband ran a tight ship. His bookkeeping records are thoroughly impressive."

The taut lines on Tammie's face softened after hearing Lucas compliment her late husband.

Journey appreciated the way Lucas was building rapport and trust with the grieving widow. His voice was soft and gentle as he guided her toward what they had come there to ask.

"We've found no indication Mr. Faulkner was in trouble of any kind...legal, financial, or otherwise. Which is great for the business but bad when we're looking to narrow down suspects and motives."

"I don't know anyone who would've wanted to hurt my... Sam." Tammie choked out her husband's name.

"That's what we're trying to figure out." Journey hoped her interjection matched Lucas's sympathetic tone. "During our investigation into Mr. Faulkner's past, we came across something of interest. Do you remember a hunting incident about seven years ago in West Virginia? It involved a man named Jerry Minton."

"Are you saying you think someone killed Sam," Tammie's voice faltered again at her husband's name, "because of what happened seven years ago?" She shifted in her chair.

Lucas shook his head. "We're just trying to understand who was close to Sam back then and if there are any connections between that group of friends and the tragedy that happened on that trip. We know the incident was ruled an accident, and no charges were filed, but we can't ignore any details that might lead us toward someone with a motive to harm your husband."

In his effort to smooth the rough edges of his question, Lucas was rambling, Journey could tell, and she worried he might be taking his empathy a little too far.

"Tammie," Journey interrupted, "we're hoping you can provide key insight on this from a personal perspective."

Closing her eyes, Tammie drew in a deep breath, as if

struggling to compose herself. "He was close with them back then. Norman, Erick, Rob, and...poor Jerry."

Journey noted the heavy sadness in Mrs. Faulkner's voice. Everything about her, from her body language to the lines in her face, spoke to the grief she still carried to this day.

Tammie's hand trembled as she grabbed a tissue box from the coffee table. "They all went on that trip to help Erick blow off some steam. He was in the middle of a nasty divorce and custody battle. Sam supplied the guns and ammunition. Norman brought the alcohol. It was supposed to be a boys' weekend, you know?"

"Alcohol and firearms, a winning combination." Lucas kept his tone low.

For her part, Journey frowned. She didn't remember any mention of alcohol in the initial report.

"I think Rob might've said something similar. They met here and loaded the car. Rob had always been a little too tightly laced, if you know what I mean." Tammie yanked a tissue from the box and wound it between her fingers. "Not a bad guy, but his good-natured advice sometimes felt a little judgmental."

"Who doesn't have a friend like that?"

"So they all left in good spirits." Journey nudged the conversation forward. "What happened after they got back?"

"They hardly saw one another after that. It was like a dark spell overtook their friendship. I can't speak for the others, but Sam just wasn't the same in the months following Jerry's death. He'd wake up in the middle of the night, and I'd find him in the kitchen, just sitting there in the dark...lost."

"Any idea why? Did he say what was bothering him?" Journey hated to see the haunted look on Tammie's face.

"I didn't know what was going on in his head. I'd ask, but Sam never wanted to get into it. Except on the rare occasion when he'd had too much to drink." Tammie pulled another tissue from the box and blotted her eyes. "Sam was a good man. I don't want you to go away thinking otherwise."

Journey tried to phrase her next questions carefully, hoping to sidestep any triggers that might shut Tammie down. "Mrs. Faulkner...Tammie, we're not here to pass judgment, nor would we, especially after he'd survived such a traumatic experience. We're just trying to suss out the facts and understand if anyone had a reason to harm your husband."

"I know. I understand." She sobbed. "But I need you to see he was a good man."

"We do." Journey's reply was soft. "We're just trying to piece everything together. Did his drinking or any other habits change after the hunting incident?"

"Why is that relevant?" Tammie's voice was low as she met Journey's gaze.

"We don't know for certain that it is." Journey matched Tammie's tone with her blunt honesty. "That's what makes Special Agent Sullivan and me good at our jobs. We know from experience that leads sometimes exist where you least expect them. Changes in behavior can have a domino effect. Especially if his new attitude rubbed off on the wrong person."

"That was seven years ago." Tammie's fist clenched around her wad of tissues. "My husband was killed a few *days* ago. His attitude after that hunting trip didn't cause that."

"How about we put a pin on that question?" Lucas held out a placating hand. "Did Sam ever tell you the details of what happened to Jerry?"

"No." Tammie took a deep breath and let out a long sigh before continuing. "It wasn't so much what he said as what he didn't say."

Lucas opened his mouth, but Journey caught his eye, shooting him a glare that said, *Give her a minute*. Tammie looked as if she were on the edge of giving them something valuable, and Journey didn't want to risk interrupting or derailing her.

Everyone fell into an uncomfortable silence as Tammie fidgeted with the crumpled tissues in her lap.

"Sam would start a thought but then leave it hanging in the air, unfinished." Her gaze dropped to the floor. "You know? He'd say things like, 'If you only knew what it was like to be there. You can't understand what it's like to see a friend die.' He looked so helpless, crushed under the overwhelming guilt of it all."

Journey waited for Tammie to continue, but the woman fell quiet and didn't seem in any rush to fill the silence. "Guilt?"

"Survivor's guilt." Tammie took another heavy breath. "I hear statements like that all the time working in senior care. It's part of the grieving process, especially when someone dies, and you think you could've done something to make their passing easier or could've prevented it entirely."

"Did Sam believe he could have prevented the accident?" Lucas beat Journey to the punch with that question.

"Obviously." Tammie scoffed. "Wouldn't you feel guilty if you witnessed a friend's death?"

"That's a very subjective question." Lucas laced his fingers together. "I might feel angry. Sad. Frightened. But not necessarily guilty. Unless I believed I was responsible."

"Sam was obsessive about firearm safety!" More tears spilled down Tammie's cheeks even as she ground her teeth together. An angry crier. "He took everything gun related seriously. He felt responsible for the safety of everyone on that trip. Now, you tell me how you think he felt when one of his own guys…his friend…didn't make it home that weekend because of one of his guns."

Journey understood Tammie's point. It didn't take a PhD

in psychology to see the connection between her own family's tragedy and her choosing a career in law enforcement. When bad things happened to the people you loved, they left a scar behind, a permanent vigilance. A warning to be sure you were prepared to protect your loved ones, no matter what.

Tammie fell back into her chair and closed her eyes. "He used to say, 'If I tell you what I saw, you'll never be able to erase it.' I guess he was trying to save me from the terrible memories he carried."

The room went quiet again as Journey noted Tammie's last thought.

Was Sam saving Tammie from trauma? Or truth?

"Thank you again, Mrs. Faulkner. We'll get out of your hair now." Lucas stood and headed toward the door.

There was definitely something behind that hunting trip worth following up on, but not with Tammie. Journey was convinced the grieving widow had given them all she knew. And pressing her further might do more damage than good.

15

Lucas and Journey spent most of Thursday morning in SSA Victoria Kenner's office, updating her on their progressing investigation. The meeting with Kenner was decent. The direction they were taking in their investigation was defendable. But the whole time, Lucas couldn't shake the sense that he wasn't quite stepping up to the job.

He'd been so focused on the details of the investigation, he hadn't noticed his hunger until he was halfway to the cafeteria and picked up on the scent of spices and cheese from the hallway. He grabbed a burrito from the counter and found an empty table in the corner.

Food usually worked to take the edge off his nerves, and he hoped that was all he needed to get his head back in the game.

Unwrapping the burrito, Lucas took a deep breath, letting the aroma of spiced meat and beans whet his palate, but when he took a bite, all he tasted was failure.

What if I'm not ready for Violent Crimes?

It seemed like such a silly thought, one his pride had been refusing to admit. But that was the heart of it. His true fear was that he'd never be capable of doing the job he'd wanted and worked for most of his life.

Maybe he'd been naive to assume his sheer desire would be motivation enough, but there was no turning back. He'd committed to the transfer. He had a new partner. Failure wasn't an option.

Lucas needed this. Not just to prove to himself that he could face his fears. He couldn't go back to White Collar Crimes. The work there had been draining his will to live.

At first, the transfer to WC had been necessary for his mental health. After his first two-year stint in Violent Crimes had left him emotionally drained and on the brink of self-destruction, it was his best hope for remaining with the FBI.

His SAC transferred him to the field office in Pittsburgh, where the change of pace and crimes he'd be investigating would be less triggering.

For a brief time, that helped, but it wasn't a magic spell.

Being closer to Serena's family provided them the support and stability they needed to ease the strain on their marriage. Lucas tried to fix things, but he'd already become an expert at driving a wedge between himself and his wife.

When Serena filed for divorce, Lucas could've taken it as a life lesson. Instead, he chose to be bitter and let his selfish anger spill over to his relationship with Hallie. He watched his daughter slip away from him, just like his marriage to her mother had.

That was when he came face-to-face with the fact that he'd become a shitty father, just like his old man.

Lucas took a morose bite of his burrito. It was spicy, making his nose run, which he wiped at with his napkin, trying to simultaneously wipe away the feelings bubbling up.

There were so many times he could've made better

choices, but he'd latched onto the darkness within himself. Instead of trying to fix things with his daughter, he left.

In retrospect, he had to.

The temporary assignment he took in the Portland Field Office was only supposed to be a six-month stint, but Lucas ended up there for three years.

That time and distance, painful as it was to be separated from his daughter, helped him in ways he couldn't have anticipated. The long, dull, mind-numbing work was just enough stimulation to keep him occupied while leaving him enough headspace to clear out some of the darkness that had been weighing him down. The hatred he felt for his father, resentment for his torpedoed marriage, and fear that every man with a gun would trigger his childhood trauma became a lighter burden.

Slowly, Lucas found his spark for life and began to rebuild.

He'd been back in Pittsburgh for six years already. He'd mended his relationship with Hallie. Made nice with Serena. Learned to be a father again.

Only he'd done all that while investigating nonviolent crimes. This case and any future ones to follow would put him face-to-face with death. He had to prove to himself, his partner, and his SAC that he could do this.

Journey found him in the cafeteria, half a burrito in. "I can't believe you eat those when there's a food truck down the block that serves unbeatable tacos."

Lucas knew good coffee but wasn't a food connoisseur. His new partner, however, had a knack for sniffing out the best local spots for every type of cuisine. "When you get hangry, you eat whatever you can."

"I hear you. This case is bugging me too. But cafeteria burritos are not the answer." She offered him one of her tacos. "Here. This'll silence the hangry monster so we can do some brainstorming."

He didn't want to take her food, but the appearance and aroma of the platter of street tacos with fresh cilantro and seasoned steak made them irresistible. When he bit into the tortilla, he knew Journey was right. He made a mental note to follow her food advice in the future.

Several bites later, Journey pushed her tray away and pulled out her notes. "I know we talked about this on the ride back to the office. I just can't shake the way Tammie Faulkner emphasized Sam's overwhelming guilt about the hunting incident." She slid her notes across the table.

At the bottom of the page, Lucas read, *Is Sam saving Tammie from trauma? Or truth?*

"Good note." He kicked himself for not zeroing in on that question earlier. "We need to dig into the full NPS case file for more details about the incident. And schedule some interviews with the other men who were on that trip."

His phone buzzed in his pocket. The caller ID read Dubovsky. He held it up to show Journey before answering.

Agent Dubovsky got straight to it. "PBP just notified us they picked up a gun with a serial number matching one stolen from Faulkner. Found it in a construction dumpster at a home under renovation a few blocks away from a case they were investigating. A case of B and E. Single fatality at the scene." He gave Lucas the relevant zone information before hanging up.

Lucas shoved his phone into his back pocket. "We'll have to hit pause on reaching out to Sam's friends. Seems we have another date with the Pittsburgh Bureau of Police."

16

Erick Lucklow stood outside his high school classroom, towering over his students as they bustled to their third-period classes. He greeted them with a wooden smile that masked the knot of nerves in his gut. "Hi, Jessica." He waved at a girl from his first period, who was walking alongside her boyfriend. "Peter. How ya doing?"

Fine, fine. Everyone was fine. Including him. Or at least, his students would think so, judging from his face, however forced his smile was.

A text message from his ex-wife had come through just five minutes earlier, telling him Norman Perry had been murdered.

His gut was screaming, but his brain fought back, ordering his other systems to stand down. He didn't know enough to freak out. But it was terrible, tragic news.

Third period was about to begin. That was his planning period, his daily free time. Soon as the bell rang, he planned to hit the internet and find as much information about Norman's death as was publicly available.

"Nice work on your midterm, Aaron." He gave a thumbs-up to a gangly teenage boy weighed down by twenty pounds of backpack. "You really knew your constitutional amendments."

The kid grinned. "I like U.S. History."

"So do I!" He related to kids like Aaron, a little physically awkward mixed with a lot of nerdy. Tall enough to play center on the basketball team but all left feet and a head in the clouds.

The bell rang. Passing time was over, but in a few hallways, stragglers still hustled toward their classes.

Erick stepped into his empty classroom and pulled the door shut behind him, taking care not to slam it, overruling his jumpy nerves.

He read Stacey's text again. *First Sam Faulkner, and now Norman Perry is dead.*

Unlike Sam's murder, which had been headline news within hours, it took a minute to find the official announcement. Norman's death elicited one brief paragraph in local news feeds.

PITTSBURGH—Norman Perry, 50, was shot and killed in a suspected home invasion Tuesday. Officers responded to reports of shots fired in the Prescott Homes neighborhood and found him dead at the scene. No further details have been released.

The article was dated the seventh of April. Erick double-checked the current date. Norman died two days after Sam.

The truth crash-landed on his chest, too heavy to breathe.

I'm next.

No. He couldn't let himself spin out.

Instead, he studied the details. Police were calling the crime a "home invasion." No mention of Sam Faulkner's death, nothing that publicly connected the two tragedies.

Only they *were* connected. Both men were friends. Hunting buddies. And both had been on the trip when Jerry Minton died. Erick knew, because he'd been there too.

And now, someone was hunting the hunters.

Erick slammed his laptop shut and stood. His heartbeat pulsed in his eardrums.

This can't be happening.

No. Maybe the murders were the result of something nefarious between Sam and Norman.

Norman was always up to something, always talking up some new million-dollar idea. At one point, Norman had tried to get him to buy doomsday prepper kits. Then there was that time he shilled for a start-up, trying to gather investors for a company that turned pig shit into bioenergy. Always working some angle, that guy.

Maybe he'd talked Sam into getting in on his latest plan, and they'd gotten in over their heads, wrapped up in something bigger than they knew, involved with the wrong people.

Now they were both dead because of it.

Erick dropped to his knees, wheezing hard and fast as he forced the breath in and out of his lungs. Nothing about this was good, but that didn't mean it was bad for him…maybe. He gasped for air until his head spun before finally forcing himself back into his chair.

Maybe he ought to go to the police. If these murders weren't some nefarious scheme gone wrong, then it could be related to that damn hunting trip. And if that was the case, the person who'd killed both Norman and Sam could be targeting everyone who was there. And if that were the case, shouldn't he do everything possible to protect himself? He had a kid. Jay was only twelve. He couldn't risk leaving his son without a father.

If he went to the authorities, he'd tell them the same story he'd recited seven years ago. Jerry had wandered into friendly fire. Because it was true. The whole thing was a tragic accident. That was what the sheriff had labeled it, and that was how it would stay.

He was just being hysterical and needed to settle down.

Rob Larson. The guy's face popped into his head. Rob, Jerry Minton's childhood friend, had also been on the trip. It was one of the many times Jerry had invited him and, as it turned out, the last.

Rob was older than the rest of them. He had a salt-and-pepper beard that sharply contrasted with his baby-faced features. Overall, though, he looked like he'd been unraveling for months. Every photo of himself he posted on social media gave a creepier vibe than the last, his hair longer, beard shaggier, skin sallower. Camouflage had become his favorite color.

After losing his job, Rob had turned into one of those guys who ranted several times a day, his messages becoming ever more deranged as the days and weeks unfolded. He railed against corporate avarice with an intensity that made Erick squirm. With each subsequent post, Erick felt himself magnetized to Rob's unfiltered anger, sensing the same rush as when witnessing a horrific crash on the highway.

When Pauline had left him, Rob's switch had really flipped as all traces of his humanity evaporated. He questioned where his morality had disappeared to and why cruelty generally came across as so fashionable these days. Rob was spiraling out of control, devoid of any sense of propriety or self-preservation.

Had seven long years of misfortune warped Rob into a killer?

Of the four witnesses on that hunting trip, only Rob had wanted to go directly to the police. Jerry, his friend, was dead. Rob's fists shook with the rage. His voice pierced the air, demanding justice for Jerry. Erick still heard it as clear as a bell to this day.

They had gone to the cops, just not the way Rob argued they should. And now he'd snapped. No job. No wife. Losing his shit every day online.

Maybe seven years of tragedy could turn a nice guy into a killer.

Get your ass over to the police station.

Erick would give them Rob's name, point out that he'd been disintegrating online for months, make the connection between him and the two murders. Authorities would have to ask how Erick knew Rob, Norm, and Sam, but he'd figure that out. Think of something. Mostly, he'd get police protection for him and his family.

Then he recalled both Sam and Norman had been shot in the stomach. Just like Jerry.

His gut churned as the truth dawned that it had to have been Rob. This killer had to be someone who was there...and everyone else was dead now. Except him and Rob.

And Rob was a superb hunter.

Before he knew he was moving, Erick leaped from his seat and sprinted toward the door, barely making it to the trash can before his stomach emptied of bile and fear.

His only thought now was escape, and he knew if he wanted to get away unseen, he had to use his sick leave. Cash it all in and flee.

The less anyone knew, the better. He was heading out of town, out of sight and out of reach.

17

I couldn't resist the thrill of hovering this close to my prey despite the risk. The thought of shooting Erick Lucklow through the gut and then bashing his skull in until it cracked open like a watermelon sent shivers down my spine.

I licked my lips as I double-checked my angles. The security cameras couldn't reach me here, lurking in the shade between my car and an ancient elm tree across the street. Only problem was, the distance had me too far away to see much. But all I needed to make out was his face. Anything that brought him into focus increased my hunger.

"You're more accomplished every day." My mother joined me, leaning against the opposite side of my car, draping her arms in that casual way that said she was in control. "You've always been brilliant, but it turns out you're strategic too."

I turned to face her. "I'm glad you're here. I miss you when you're not around."

"You've been busy. Best not to get in your way." She came around to my side of the vehicle.

We stood quietly for a moment, studying each other.

"Am I losing my mind?"

Her pencil-thin eyebrows went straight up. "Where is this coming from?"

"I don't know. I was just..." I dropped my gaze to the dirt, ashamed of my weakness. I kept staring down for so long, it became humiliating. I couldn't bring myself to look at her. "This mission. What if I fail? What then?"

"What if I fail?" She mocked me in a whiny, little boy voice. "I don't want to hear any of that *poor-me* crap. Life gets tough. But that's when you find out what you're made of. You can either lie down and die of self-pity or steel your spine and right some wrongs."

"But...what if—"

"Snap out of it." She stomped her foot. "You won't fail because you're doing righteous work. You gave Noah, Sam, and Norman what they deserved. More men await their justice, and you will deliver." She squared her face with mine. "Look at me."

I couldn't.

"Look at me, dammit!"

"What?" Fear turned to rage in my throat. "What do you want from me? I told you I'd finish the job, so I'll finish the job."

"No." She stomped again. "You will *avenge*. Your power grows with every life you take. These are evil men who no longer deserve space on this earth or oxygen to breathe."

She paused. I knew she wanted me to acknowledge what she'd said, but I was pouting. Acting the part of the small boy she saw me as. I wanted her there, but seeing her had put me in a funk. Her expectations were too high, the risk of disappointing her suddenly too real.

"I want to do this." I swallowed my emotions, forcing them down. My voice came out like a croaking whisper. "That's why I'm here. Because I am the bringer of justice. I have a duty to bring an end to their evil existence. They deserve justice, and I will bring it, without mercy." A wave of emotion surged within me, and I was frozen in its intensity. My fingers curled into tight fists, and my heart galloped.

My mother's face lit up, her lips lifting into a satisfied grin. "That's my boy."

Across the street, the door leading out to the parking lot opened, and a man stepped through. I studied his face, but he was too far away to be sure.

"I'm sorry. I've got to go." I grabbed my keys from my pocket and threw open the door to the car. Instinct was telling me otherwise.

No time to dwell. The man who exited the building was my guy, even though it didn't make sense why he was leaving in the middle of the day. My clock said quarter to noon.

What's he up to?

I'd been surveying the area from the lot across the street for three days now.

Erick jumped into his silver Ford Escape and took a left out of the lot.

I followed, careful to stay several car lengths behind, but as soon as we got off the side streets and onto the highway, it became easier to keep him in view.

Ten minutes later, he pulled into his driveway, opened the garage door, and disappeared inside.

I parked in the first available spot across the street and adjusted my position so I could see his house more clearly.

A knock at my window had me nearly jumping out of my seat. Startled, I looked up to find an elderly man peering in. I cracked the window.

He wore a thick but pilled cardigan the color of dirty water, and the murky whites of his eyes showed signs of poor health. "Can I help you with something, young man? You're sitting outside my house. I have the right to know what you're up to."

"I pulled over to look something up. Safety first." I held up my phone, careful not to display the blank screen. I rolled my window back up.

The man knocked on the window again, harder this time. "You can go do that somewhere else. Go on, get!"

Dammit!

Even if the street was public property, I couldn't have this old man hanging around while I watched Erick. I cranked the ignition and threw the car in drive, peeling out and not caring whether I drove over the guy's foot.

Pain in the ass old man.

I drove until he disappeared from view, found the nearest parking lot, and killed the engine.

Focus.

This was nothing more than a brief setback.

Today wouldn't be my reunion with the man I'd been hunting, but I'd be back.

And when I return, no one will see me coming.

18

A few hours later—the soonest they could get Detective Patty Traynor in a room—Journey and Lucas sat side by side in the Zone One Police Station conference room, a long table separating them and the hard-to-reach detective.

"Had it not been for the serial number on the gun found in the dumpster, Norman Perry and Sam Faulkner's murders wouldn't have been connected so quickly." Patty riffled through pages spread out in front of her.

Journey watched her, already making connections. Norman Perry was one of the men who'd gone on that hunting trip with Sam Faulkner seven years ago. That made two from that group who were now dead, three with Faulkner. Add Noah Hudson, the park ranger from the scene of the original incident, and it added up to way more than a coincidence.

"The injuries were similar to Faulkner's, but that isn't uncommon in a robbery." Patty finished digging through her papers. "And the distance between the two crimes didn't raise any suspicion. An experienced perp would know that spreading their crimes across jurisdictions would slow an investigation's progress."

"I wouldn't give him or her too much credit." Lucas leaned forward in his chair, arms resting on the table edge. "They didn't think about the serial numbers on the gun being traceable."

"Fair point." Patty nodded. "Thank ATF for that."

"How did you locate the weapon?"

"Thought the perp was a meth head. That's what I've been dealing with all afternoon. We've seen this kind of stash-and-run move before, so I had a few people canvass the neighborhood and check things like dumpsters and trash." Patty paused and gave Journey a pointed look. "You'd be amazed by how many times a murderer throws away their weapon when they think it'll disappear in a landfill."

Journey gave a grim, tight-lipped nod in response. The detective was right. Criminals were oftentimes not the brightest.

"What made you think this one was amphetamine related?" Lucas shifted his weight and raised his eyebrows. "You've had other drug-related robberies in the neighborhood?"

"Perry lived in an upscale neighborhood. The area has a pretty low crime rate, but meth has been changing all the rules. Can't really ever tell where it'll hit next. More addicts need more money, which means they expand their target areas. You know how it goes."

"Sure do. Meth turns people crazy. And the addiction will make them do anything for that next hit." Journey knew just how dangerous the drug could be from firsthand experience in the Las Vegas Field Office. Clark County had a sizable meth problem. The drug was cheaper than cocaine or heroin, which allowed it to spread faster. And with Mexico pumping out purer product by the day, the number of users kept increasing.

"You get it." Patty smiled. "So we had a team search the area for the murder weapon. Sure enough, found it in a construction dumpster a couple blocks away from Norman Perry's house. Still waiting on ballistics report to match the gun with Perry's wound. But as soon as we entered the serial number, it pinged ATF, and we knew it was one of Faulkner's."

"What do you know about Perry's home security situation?" Lucas glanced through a paperclipped packet of documents.

"Power was cut to the house, and he didn't appear to have a backup generator, so we've got nothing there." Patty slid the report across the conference table to Journey. "This is what we have so far on the crime scene. Still waiting on a few things, but we'll let you know when we have something more."

Journey flipped to the section that described the scene when officers arrived. Kitchen cupboards and bedroom drawers turned upside down. The BMW still in the garage. They found Norman's wallet beside his body, empty of cash, but the credit card slots were full.

"And Perry's body was found in the basement, correct?"

"I think you'll note it's a pretty familiar set of circumstances. The power was out when officers arrived on scene. Perry was probably heading down to the fuse box. The window in the basement was open, so we estimate that's where the perp ambushed Perry. Got off a single shot to the stomach. Maybe Perry fought a little, and they were so high they lost the gun. That's another reason we suspected amphetamines." Patty mimed smacking her head. "Skull trauma. The perp smashed that poor guy's head in with a rock."

Journey knew that a person functioning on amphetamines had bottomless energy, and every idea that popped into their head was considered a spark of genius sent directly from the heavens above.

The detective went on. "I'm telling you. That new meth on the streets now isn't just getting people high. It's leading to meth-induced psychosis too. We're picking up users who are so tweaked out, they don't know who they are days and weeks after using. I had the 'queen of ancient Egypt' in custody last week. She'd just walked out of her shift at a day care center and smashed up a beauty salon."

Back in Las Vegas, Journey had been playing poker in a local casino by her apartment. She'd overheard a guy, obviously high as a kite, a few tables over screaming about God showing him the winning hand. Next thing, that man flew across a table. He kept screaming about God as he tried to choke out the poor dealer. It took four security officers to pull him off the dealer and the table, and even then, they struggled to get him up and off the casino floor.

If they were dealing with a big meth problem in the area, Journey understood why the detective might be busy. But she didn't buy that the detective would think these deaths related to the street situation.

"Sam Faulkner and Norman Perry have a shared history. We don't believe this string of homicides is related to the meth situation." She proceeded to explain what they knew about Sam Faulkner, Norman Perry, Jerry Minton, and their connection to Noah Hudson.

The detective, while clearly tired, accepted their point of view. She took notes and said she would keep an eye out for further connections.

On the ride back to the field office, Journey rubbed her gold ace of diamonds pendant for luck as her mind raced with theories. "We've got two of the five men who went on that hunting trip murdered in the space of a couple days. Both homicides linked by the same fatal injuries."

"And the ranger from West Virginia," Lucas added, his eyes flitting toward Journey for a split second. "Whose death investigation details we still need to pull."

"Right." Journey sighed heavily. "We do know that Hudson was around when that hunting accident happened. The incident report I saw put him there. But I'm waiting on the full file to be sent over."

Lucas glanced at her once again. "Are you thinking these might be revenge killings?"

"After seven years? I don't know." Journey shrugged. "Why wait so long?"

"Maybe our perp was incarcerated." He pulled the car into the field office parking lot and drove around it, finding an open space next to Journey's red Mazda. "If that's the case, they wouldn't be able to do anything until being released."

She considered that for a moment. "Something to look into while we're checking on the other men from the hunting trip." She opened her door but paused and glanced back at Lucas before stepping out. "Thanks for the ride back. See you bright and early tomorrow morning. Be ready to do some digging."

19

As Lucas drove home, his mind raced with thoughts of the recent murder of Norman Perry. Even though Journey had made a connection between Sam Faulkner and Noah Hudson, they'd been too late to the game to look into the other men who'd gone on the trip. Could he have prevented Norman Perry's death if they'd made the connection sooner?

This was always the struggle with every case.

But he couldn't think like that. They were investigating this case to the best of their ability. Blaming himself for not connecting dots they weren't yet privy to wasn't going to solve the case. He had to shut off the inner voice that found blame and shame where none existed.

There was still a lot of work to be done. Sleep was what Lucas needed. A good night of rest would provide clarity of thought, but as Lucas pulled into his driveway, he recognized his restless mind and nervous energy were sure to make sleep impossible.

Frustrated, he began cleaning his home. Lucas scrubbed the toilets, wiped the mirrors, and bleached the bathroom and kitchen sinks.

Room after room passed beneath his cleaning supplies. His meticulous search for every dust bunny and streak of soap scum usually proved to be the perfect way to distract himself from the noise in his head. But no matter how hard he tried, Lucas kept thinking about the serial killer they were chasing and how desperately they needed to make an arrest before more lives were taken.

He had half a mind to head back to the field office and start researching. But all-nighters never ended well. Maybe when he was in his twenties, but something had changed after his thirtieth birthday. And regardless of his intentions or copious amounts of coffee, he would crash at some point.

And the last thing he needed was for Journey to catch him snoring at his desk.

Just the thought of that stoked his anxiety and sent him into Hallie's room, searching for more things to clean. He pulled off her comforter and threw it into the wash on the hottest cycle, all the while thanking his lucky stars that Hallie was at her mom's house. She hated when he turned into "Neurotic Mr. Clean," as she lovingly called him.

He'd earned the moniker for sure this time. It was well past midnight by the time he finished scrubbing the grout in the shower. Lucas had to work himself into full exhaustion if he wanted to get any sleep.

It was one of those nights.

The tile and grout glistened, and Lucas's biceps ached from scrubbing. He stripped off his wet clothes, pulled a t-shirt over his head, found a clean pair of flannel joggers in his drawer, and fell into bed, letting the physical exhaustion turn into a dreamless sleep.

It seemed as if Lucas had only just closed his eyes, but the incessant beep of his alarm at quarter to six said otherwise. He woke Friday to a dawning light without sun. He'd slept several hours, but like the gray mist fogging his bedroom windows, morning arrived without clarity, and an equal bleakness settled over him.

Time to get on with it.

He forced himself out of bed and pulled on a crisp white shirt and a navy blue blazer before heading downstairs to brew the strongest coffee in his cabinet. He would need all the mentally stimulating effects caffeine could offer.

Today needed to be productive.

He arrived at the FBI field office at seven fifteen. Later than he would've liked but still early enough to get plenty of work done. As he stepped off the elevator into the fourth-floor bullpen, he scanned the room until his gaze landed on Journey sitting at their double-desk workspace in the back corner.

She flashed him a wide grin as he approached and handed him a steaming mug of black coffee. "French roast, two sugars, no cream."

"Wow." He was genuinely touched. "Thank you."

"I had to get up extra early to get that." She yawned so wide, he glimpsed her back molars. "Which means I must enjoy being your partner because I don't do extra early for just anyone."

He took a sip. The roast was deep and rich, the way he liked it. "Tastes expensive."

Her smirk confirmed as much. "I got it from the gourmet roaster around the corner from my apartment. A half pound of beans cost me about a half month's rent. So drink up, because when this is gone…" She whistled the fading peal of a bomb falling to earth.

He laughed. His new partner not only knew about local

cuisine but also had the info on a great cup of joe. "I *extra* appreciate it, then."

The murder wall in their corner of the bullpen was slowly filling up. Lucas noted a change since yesterday—Journey had added Norman Perry to the board and moved a few things around. He studied her. "What are you working on?"

She held up the Norman Perry folder. "Let's start with ballistics." She slid a copy of the report onto his desk. "They confirmed the gun found in a construction dumpster two blocks away from Perry's residence was the same weapon used to kill him. A Sig Sauer P three sixty-five."

He scanned the findings as she spoke, his heart quickening. *This just might be a good day after all.*

Journey slumped into her chair. "Unfortunately, forensics didn't find any prints on it."

So much for getting my hopes up.

Finding a print would be too easy, of course. The universe needed to balance itself, to throw bad news in with the good. "Meaning we know where the gun came from but not who used it."

"Not yet." She popped up from her seat again and stuck a yellow sticky note on the far side of the murder board, where Norman Perry's name had been added. The note read, *Ballistics = SS P365 from FG&A.*

Lucas linked his hands behind his head. "Anything else?"

"Yep." She slid another report across the desks. "They also told me something that wasn't in the initial report we received. Apparently, Pittsburgh Bureau of Police lab analysis came back, and they found blood on Perry's sleeve. It's type O positive. But Perry was B negative."

He sat up straight, reaching for the report. "Actual blood, or flakes like from Faulker's crime scene?"

"Actual."

She returned to her desk and reached for the folder

containing the Pittsburgh Bureau of Police crime scene analysis. Scribbling on another sticky note, she stuck it inside the cover. "Police think the blood is from the assailant."

That made sense. "Know anything more?"

"Just that it's from a male. The lab has expedited DNA analysis and promised to have it ready for us ASAP. We might get lucky and get a hit."

This time, Lucas grabbed the stack of tiny sticky notes. He scribbled on one and stuck it under the note Journey had posted.

It read, *Male suspect.*

"It's a small win, and we kinda figured it was a dude before, but I'll take it." They had a male at the scene of the Norman Perry murder and a male on security footage outside Sam Faulkner's. Two men murdered in the same fashion, with guns linked to the same shop. "What's that they say? Every avalanche starts with just one flake?"

Journey laughed. "Not sure that's how the saying goes, but I like the attitude."

Something was shifting. Lucas sensed it.

20

Journey and Lucas had been hunkered down in their little corner of Violent Crimes all morning, leaving their desks only long enough to refill their coffees. On Journey's way back from her third fill-up of the morning, her computer pinged with a new email notification. "Looks like the lab finished the analysis of the blood found at the scene of Norman Perry's murder."

"Oh, yeah." Lucas was looking at his computer, his voice suggesting he'd seen the same email.

She clicked, scanned the results, and sat back, deflated. "Did you read the finding from the lab?"

Lucas grimaced. "No matches."

While the forensic lab had managed to run a complete screen on the blood, they hadn't found a match in NGI, the FBI's biometric database.

"I hate it when that happens."

Another inbox *ping*, and Journey spied a message indicating the Pittsburgh Bureau of Police had updated the case file. "Got an update from PBP." She clicked and read aloud. "Officers finished canvassing Perry's neighborhood, but no one recalled witnessing a break-in."

"With news like that, we should be about ready for the parlor room scene."

Journey's chuckle matched Lucas's grim tone.

With little for them to follow up on, Journey pulled up the information on the two men they still needed to check into. Erick Lucklow and Rob Larson were the last two men connected to the hunting trip where Jerry Minton had been killed. Now that three homicides connected to that trip, Journey and Lucas couldn't wait any longer to speak with them.

After Journey jotted down their addresses, curiosity flashed through her.

She did a little social media scrolling to see what she could find on the two remaining men from the hunting trip. Neither she nor Lucas suspected them to be the one selling Faulkner's guns, but since they planned on checking in with them, it wouldn't hurt to get a little background info on Erick Lucklow and Rob Larson before heading out.

Journey started with Lucklow, hoping there weren't too many guys with his unique spelling combination. Three cheers for parents who made their kids easier to find online by ensuring their names stood out from those of their peers.

There he was, a forty-something man with a thin face, friendly smile, and glasses. Lucklow was a high school history teacher, and he looked the part. Aside from the unassuming Mr. Rogers wardrobe, he was taller than almost everyone in his photos. He had to be six-four or six-five. More than just tall, he towered over his peers. But other than a few posts about awards or requests for school fundraisers, Lucklow posted nothing personal. Journey decided to move on to Rob Larson.

She said a silent prayer that Lucklow wasn't a stickler

about security settings and clicked on his friend list, hoping he and Rob were still connected.

It worked. All six hundred and thirteen of his friends' names were available for searching. Scrolling quickly, she dove straight in toward the Ls.

Robert Banes Larson.

Robert Michael Larson.

Two Robert Larsons. At first, she worried about having to ensure she had the correct man. Then she saw that Robert Banes Larson was just a kid, his profile filled with stills of his online game triumphs.

Robert Michael Larson's profile featured a picture of a guy in blaze orange, kneeling next to a dead six-pointer.

Unlike Erick's bland profile, which lacked any personal information, Robert's was like an unfiltered stream of consciousness, including religious fervor and hate speech. In one breath, he touted the decline of family values, and in the next, he spouted off about defunding the police.

Journey scrolled past a photo of Robert wearing a hoodie and dark jeans. With his hair covered by the hood, he looked sketchy. She made note of that as well as the number of photos showing Robert and his guns.

Lucas's phone vibrated on the desk. "Text from Dubovsky ATF. This might be something. Last night, Pittsburgh Bureau of Police arrested a man named Emmett Cohen for armed robbery, and when they ran the serial number on his weapon, it matched one of the guns stolen from Faulkner's Guns & Ammo."

"Give me a sec to make a request for PBP to do a wellness check on our two guys from the hunting trip, and then let's go." After hours of doing quiet research and feeling like they were getting nowhere fast, Journey was eager to have something worth following up on. She grabbed her car keys. "Which zone? Same one as the Perry murder?"

Lucas stood, preparing to follow. "No, different one, but they've still got him in custody."

With her brief burst of adrenaline already flatlining, Journey slipped her keys back into her pocket. "You drive."

The police station was a flurry of activity, every chair in the waiting room filled with anxious faces. A woman in a winter coat and flannel pajama bottoms fed a baggie of cereal to her hungry toddler as she shouted into her cell phone. An older woman sat beside her, her lips silently working over prayers on the rosary beads she clutched between her fingers. A young man slouched in his seat, eyes closed, seemingly unfazed by the surrounding chaos.

Journey strode up to the front desk and asked to speak with the arresting officer on the Emmett Cohen case.

As they waited, Lucas unwrapped a piece of gum and offered it to Journey. "I've got coffee breath."

She took the gum with an amused smirk. "You trying to tell me something?" But before he had time to answer, they were buzzed through to an inner office.

Inside, they met Officer Martin, a man with gray temples, biceps bulging within his uniform, and a waistline thickened with age.

When Journey and Lucas flashed their IDs, Martin nodded at Journey's introduction but didn't offer his hand or a first name.

Journey went on, refusing to acknowledge the slight. "We understand you have a man in custody by the name of Emmett Cohen and that the weapon in his possession at the time of arrest matches the serial number of one stolen from Faulkner's Guns and Ammo."

Martin dropped his head and shook it—the behavior of

an exasperated man. "If you Feds plan to show up every time we get an attempted armed robbery that turns up a stolen weapon, you better clear your calendars."

Lucas didn't pause to marinate in Martin's sarcasm. "You got more stolen guns we should know about?"

"You got a reason I need to spend time briefing you on Cohen?" Martin flicked his chin toward the waiting room. "It's mayhem in here today, in case you haven't noticed."

Journey stepped farther down the hall, forcing Martin and Lucas to follow her into the depths of the station. "You have a room where we can talk?"

"Convince me that right here's not a good place to hear what you've got to say, and maybe I'll go find one."

She studied Martin's face, trying to get a read on him. Cool receptions like his no longer shocked her. Not like when she was a new agent, young and green and eager to please. In her nearly ten years with the Bureau, she'd learned that the first step in weaseling into a resistant officer's good graces was to figure out which variety of bug was up their ass.

A few officers were just assholes. Acting like that was a lousy way to spend a life, so at least she wasn't doomed to such an existence herself.

Martin checked his watch and huffed, leading her to suspect he was just a jerk with too much to do.

She got straight to the point. "Look, from what ATF told us, you're holding Cohen for a robbery in which nobody was hurt. But we're looking for the perpetrator of two premeditated murders and the thief of several firearms, one of which was used by your suspect. The quicker you get us in to chat with your guy, the quicker we get out of your hair."

Still scowling, Martin led them down the hallway.

21

Journey and Lucas read over the file Officer Martin had provided as they sat in the stark interview room, waiting for Emmett Cohen to be escorted in.

The room was more closet than interrogation space, with soundproof walls—perhaps white at some point—dingy and yellow with age. They clearly had seen better days. One wall held a panel of mirrored glass. Officer Martin was most likely on the other side so he could monitor their conversation.

The furniture was bolted to the floor, forcing Journey to adjust her position on the chair's edge for a good look at the file spread out between her and her partner.

An intriguing point struck Journey's attention as she perused. "After robbing an antique store at gunpoint, Emmett Cohen had nearly two thousand dollars of cash in his pockets. But when police arrived, he willingly set down his weapon and allowed himself to be taken into custody without resisting. Why would he do that?"

"Something we'll have to figure out. But we can't just jump right off with that."

"I'll let you take the lead on questions. Depending on Cohen's attitude, I can adapt my style to gain his cooperation."

Before Lucas could agree, the door opened, and uniformed officers escorted Emmett Cohen into the interview room. He was a middle-aged man who'd seen better days. Ratty jeans hung loosely from his too-thin frame, and the gray t-shirt was more like a crop top, too short to hide his hairy navel. Despite his shabby appearance, he had an abundance of thick, black hair, making him luckier than about half of the men in his age-group.

As soon as Emmett sat down, he started talking. "You know I didn't hurt anyone, right? Because I didn't. It was stupid. What the hell was I thinking? Of course they had an alarm. Story of my effed up life. Cripes, I'm stupid."

His forehead beaded with sweat.

Lucas held up a palm to silence Cohen's rambling as he made a show of looking over the police report Officer Martin had given them. "Says here you held up an antique store." He met Cohen's eyes dead-on. "Why'd you choose this target?"

"I needed the money." Cohen couldn't hold Lucas's stare. His gaze darted around the room. "There's a sign on the door that says *Cash Only*. The place seemed like an easy target."

"Had you been watching the place?" Lucas set the file down and folded his hands on top of it, still keeping his gaze on Cohen.

"No." Cohen shook his head. "I just saw the sign one day and got the idea."

"How's that?" Lucas's eyebrow arched with curiosity.

"Didn't he tell you this already?" Cohen gestured toward the one-way mirror. "I got the gun on Monday for self-defense. I didn't want to, but I had to borrow money from the kind of guy you never want to be in debt to, and I've been having trouble paying it back." He grabbed his hair by the roots and tugged, a man punishing himself. "I don't want to die on account of a few thousand dollars."

"So you borrowed money from the wrong people and bought a gun to defend yourself when you couldn't pay it back?"

"I mean. Yeah, that's the short version." Cohen nodded and dropped his gaze to the floor.

"Enlighten us then."

"When I got released from Frackville in October, I had nothin'. My buddy let me crash on his couch, and his mom loaned me some cash while I got back on my feet. And things were startin' to look up. I was workin' at a gas station round the corner, and just when I had enough money saved up, my buddy calls me from the hospital. His mom started bleedin', and they found out she had cancer. He couldn't afford all her treatments, so I offered to help however I could...for her, you know? She's a good woman. Nobody deserves cancer."

Journey watched Cohen as he shifted in his seat and ran a hand through his short hair. It was a good story, true or not. She didn't know enough to judge him yet.

"So I had to pull together some funds. I know you're gonna ask me who I owed." Cohen averted his gaze again. "But I'm not gonna tell you, so don't bother."

Lucas shook his head. "Actually, we're more interested in what you did than why."

Journey shot him a side-eyed glance. She was interested in the why. Digging into motivation often yielded details she wouldn't think to ask about otherwise. But Lucas was leading this round.

At least, for now.

Cohen tugged at his hair again. "I told you. I got the gun on Monday to defend myself. I was late paying my loan back and was convinced this guy's crew was coming after me any day. And I was walking to work one morning and noticed the *Cash Only* sign on the antique store. So I got to thinking about how easy it would be to just go in and get the job done. Like a smash-and-grab."

"So yesterday you go in. Hold the place up. Grab the cash and plan to run." Lucas filled in the blanks from the info in the police report.

"Yep." Cohen nodded with a sigh of resignation. "But like I said, I didn't expect they'd have an alarm button. I mean, shit, anyone else in the neighborhood calls the cops. It takes 'em an hour to get there. But these fancy guys press a tiny button, and wham."

Lucas sat back. He didn't speak, just snapped the clasp on his watch. Open, shut. Open, shut. It was his tic, a habit when he was working through something in his mind. Journey didn't know whether to interpret it as good or bad just yet.

Meanwhile, the questions Journey kept to herself became a twenty-car pileup in her brain. *Ask him about buying the gun. Get a description of the seller. We already know the information documented in the police report.*

Another few seconds, and the echo of Lucas clicking the watch clasp became too much to tolerate.

Journey's brow furrowed as she studied Lucas's and Cohen's expressions, her patience worn thin from lack of sleep. "Tell me about the guy who sold you the gun." She set down her pen and mirrored Cohen's posture. "You said in your statement that you bought the gun off the street."

"Yeah." Cohen nodded. "I asked around. Somebody said they knew a guy who was selling to move. You know, priced his inventory cheap so he didn't have it hanging around too long."

Journey leaned forward slightly with interest. "And this is the same gun you used in the robbery?"

Cohen nodded.

Lucas stopped clicking his watch band. "You said a friend put you in touch?"

"No." Cohen shook his head. "I said 'somebody.' Everybody I know is hooked up somehow. A friend of a friend's cousin. That kind of thing."

"Okay. What can you tell us about him?" Even as she asked, Journey noted Lucas's distraction. "The guy who sold you the gun?"

"He was just some guy." Cohen hesitated with a shrug before continuing. "Antsy. Inexperienced…I guess."

"What makes you say that?" Journey's eyes narrowed as she watched Cohen's body language.

"I don't know guns well. I'm not all that street. Okay?" Cohen's gaze darted all over the room, as if he wanted to look anywhere except at Journey. "I told him I needed something small. He showed me the only gun he had with him. And he seemed eager to sell. He told me two fifty. I know that's a good price, so I didn't haggle with him. He took my money without even counting it and disappeared."

That certainly sounded like inexperience to Journey's ears. And though Cohen seemed evasive, she believed he was being on the level. Given his recent incarceration and the cooperation he'd shown the arresting officers, not to mention his open admission of so much during their conversation, clearly Cohen understood the benefit of playing nice.

Journey had an idea. A way to get a bit more out of him. But first, she needed to see if Officer Martin would play ball. "Time for a five-minute break."

"Just you?" Lucas raised a curious eyebrow. "Or are we all taking a break?"

"Just follow me." Journey nodded toward the door.

They walked down the hall and entered the observation

room on the other side of the one-way mirror, where Officer Martin was standing.

"He's not our guy." Journey made her pronouncement before anyone else had the chance to speak. "Nothing about him says two-time murderer."

Lucas crossed his arms, not looking especially convinced. He turned to Martin. "What do you think of Cohen's story?"

"He told us the same thing." Martin slid off the corner of the desk and sauntered over to join them, looking through the glass at Cohen as he spoke. "And the details check out. Released on parole in October. Nonviolent offense. Reportedly violation free until this weekend. Arresting officers said he put down the gun and hit the floor as soon as he saw them enter. Kept yelling that he didn't want any trouble."

Journey paced back and forth, skimming her notes in a flurry. "Anyone followed up with the buddy, the one whose mom supposedly has cancer and needed the money?"

Martin gave a quick nod. "Spoke with her oncologist too. Advanced colon cancer."

"Sounds like a death sentence." Lucas rapped his knuckles on the doorjamb. "So his story checks out."

"Right. So we can reasonably assume he's telling the truth. And that gun can be traced to one stolen from Faulkner." Journey looked at Martin and Lucas, waiting for someone to get on the same wavelength before continuing. After a moment of silence, she decided to just spell it out for them. "He bought it face-to-face from the seller."

The penny dropped for Lucas. "The seller who got the gun during the Faulkner murder. You think Cohen dealt with our killer." His brow furrowed. "But he didn't have much to say about the guy who sold him the gun. *Antsy* isn't much of description to go on."

"Maybe his memory needs a little incentive." Journey

waggled her eyebrows at Martin. "You think the D.A. is in the mood to negotiate?"

Martin was stone-faced.

"Cohen seems willing to cooperate." Journey pressed. "He just might need a little encouragement. So maybe the D.A. can come up with something in exchange for a sketch of the gun seller."

Lucas's eyes locked with Journey's, and he held the gaze for a beat. "Yeah. Might work." He aimed his own puppy-dog gaze at Martin.

Martin let out a heavy sigh, more irritated than charmed, Journey was sure. "The D.A. will worry about accusations of being soft on crime."

"I hear that. But, even if Cohen wasn't speaking to our perpetrator, he can give us a decent idea of who's selling those guns. That's going to help get dangerous weapons off the street and might stop a potential serial killer at the same time." Journey hoped that suggestion might make Officer Martin a little more willing to make some calls.

Martin snorted, but he picked up his phone.

22

Journey met Lucas in the office parking garage early on Saturday morning. They were among the first people to arrive and ended up parking side by side on the ground level next to the front door.

She carried a single travel mug of fresh coffee, as did Lucas. Neither had brought drinks for their partner.

Lucas got to the door before her and held it open. Too much perk in his step to be anything but annoying. "Good night?"

"Nope. You?"

He raised an eyebrow and paused a beat before answering. "Uh, yeah, actually. My daughter, Hallie, was with me. We went to a movie. Got some takeout."

Journey skipped the elevator in favor of the stairs, too amped to stand still in a three-by-six box. She reached the stairwell and didn't wait for him to follow before launching herself, two steps at a time, toward the fourth floor.

Lucas's voice echoed up the stairwell from behind her. "Something bothering you?"

"Nope." Journey kept her answer short, not wanting to go into details.

She'd come home from work, thrown a frozen pizza in the oven, and crashed onto the couch to watch the news while it baked. An hour later, she woke in a panic from a dream about a burning house. She rushed to the oven, turned the heat off, and opened the door. Smoke billowed out, setting off the fire alarm, and the pizza was burned black.

By the time the air cleared, she was in tears, gripped by decades-old fear and anger.

The apartment wasn't on fire, but to a mind scarred by the trauma of having witnessed a real tragedy by fire, it might as well have been. She'd choked back the scream in her throat milliseconds before letting it go.

To anyone else, burning a pizza would be little more than a careless mistake. To the damaged little girl inside her, it was a reminder that nothing, not even home, life, or family, was safe. A fact proved true once again when her sister, Michelle, nearly died.

Two years earlier, a colleague kidnapped, raped, and physically abused Michelle, and it had taken more than a year of intense physical and emotional therapy for her to find her feet again. Michelle was back at work now and living alone, but she still functioned a few notches above survival mode. Eventually, she'd be capable of more, but for now, day by day was enough.

Until that changed, Journey would deal with her ancient issues by herself. And admittedly, how she did so was often for the worse, not the better. No need to rope in Michelle or anyone else.

"You sure? You're okay? Because you're usually more talkative."

They hit the third-floor landing, where she stopped just long enough to answer. "I don't like waiting on evidence."

"Ah." Lucas nodded as if he understood.

She doubted that.

Emmett Cohen had made a deal with Sally Fray, the Allegheny County D.A. In exchange for reduced charges on attempted armed robbery, he'd cooperated with the police artist to construct a sketch of the man who'd sold him the gun and would testify against him when apprehended.

As Journey made her way to their desks, Lucas began collecting the copies from the printer.

His expression wasn't encouraging.

Journey grabbed her copy of the sketch and studied it, then pulled it up on her computer and zoomed in for a better look.

The man in the sketch had a square face with no distinguishing features. No tattoos, no scars, an average boy-next-door chin. His hair, which Cohen had described as brownish, was trim, not too short but not shaggy. He had an unruly cowlick where his part swirled into a circle on top of his head, making some hairs at the back stand straight up.

Journey's free hand wandered to her own hair. "Makes you wonder...bad barber or bad luck in the genetic lottery?"

Cohen also described him as white, somewhere in his mid-twenties, maybe five feet, ten inches tall. He'd worn a black sweatshirt and jeans. Too bad Cohen hadn't thought to notice his shoes.

"He looks like he could be anyone. The guy standing in line behind me at Java Joint or the grocery store." Journey tossed the sketch onto her desk. This wasn't the way she wanted their day to begin.

Lucas chuckled. "There's always a chance someone might recognize him."

"Sure. Good old Generic John Doe has friends somewhere, right?"

"I was thinking more like sending out a BOLO."

Despite her foul mood, Journey agreed. "We should also check the state and national databases for suspects matching the same physical description."

"Goes without saying." Lucas set his elbows on the desk and rested his chin on his hands. "Speaking of things we're not saying, I think we ought to talk about what happened yesterday."

"Yesterday?" Journey suddenly had the feeling she and Lucas were in a relationship and about to have *the talk*.

"At the precinct. You cut off the interview with Cohen, then went after a deal for Martin without consulting me." His voice was firm but neutral.

Clearly, he's been thinking about how to broach the subject.

Journey's mind tripped over one word. "Consult you?"

"Yeah." He crossed his arms and pushed back from the desk but kept his expression flat.

"As in…ask your permission?" Journey's eyebrows began to rise. "For doing my job."

"Permission? No." Lucas scoffed. "We're partners. On the same team, right? Just, like, give me a heads-up. We'd agreed on tactics, then you stepped out. You shut Cohen down and marched straight out of the room. Expected me to follow you like a dog."

"I don't think that's fair. I saw an opportunity. You seemed distracted. Just clicking your watch."

"You've got to leave some silence. The suspect will often rush to fill it, trying to explain themselves. The watch clicking helps them understand time is going by. It's a niggling in their brain. You cut through that strategy."

"I didn't know that was the strategy." She paused, realizing Lucas's strategy had actually worked on her. His clasping and silence had niggled her into interrupting. "I saw an opportunity and made a judgment call in the moment. We all do that." Irritated, Journey struggled to keep her attitude in check. She understood what Lucas was getting at, but if the situation had been reversed, she wouldn't have gotten as bent out of shape about it. "And I figured my partner would have my back."

"I do. I caught what you threw." He nodded. "But if we're going to make this work," he wagged his finger between them, "we're going to have to communicate...at least until we learn each other's cues and styles."

Yeah, this is definitely the talk.

"Go on."

"I can't read your mind." Lucas tapped his forehead. "Which means I can't back you up if I don't know what you're doing."

That was the same argument she and Michelle had more often than Journey wanted to admit. Only, Michelle was the more likely of the two to go silent, to refuse to share her thoughts and bottle up her emotions. Now Lucas was accusing Journey of something along those lines.

He leaned in and gently knocked on the desk to regain her attention. "Hey, I'm not trying to start something here. I just want to keep our work together on the right side of functional."

"You're right." Journey sighed. "Thanks, I guess, for bringing it up. But this is a two-way street. You've got to tell me your tactic before going in, so I don't jump all over you. And I'll try to be more transparent."

"Me too. And don't hesitate to call me out if I'm not." He gave her a nod and turned his attention to the computer. "I'm going to get that BOLO issued."

"Great." Journey grabbed her phone and keys from the desk. "And then let's go pay a visit to our hunters, Erick Lucklow and Robert Larson."

"Didn't you have PBP check on them?"

"According to the message I got from our contact, Patty Traynor," she sighed, "there was no answer at either residence."

23

Journey's stomach growled as they walked up Erick Lucklow's driveway. It was almost noon, and she'd had nothing aside from coffee that morning.

Mr. Lucklow's brick bungalow was in a typical suburban Pittsburgh working-class neighborhood, peaceful during midday. Trees were healthy and stood tall. Birds chirped happily among the canopy of leaves and branches. Most of the driveways and curbside parking spots were empty. Hardly a car passed as they headed up the steps to the porch.

Lucas knocked and stepped back to join Journey on the small cement stoop.

As they waited, Journey spotted a pair of squirrels scurrying across the yard, heading for a bird feeder hanging from the porch next door.

There was no answer at Lucklow's door, so Lucas tried again, leaning into the doorbell this time. He held it for several long seconds before adding a few insistent knocks. "Erick Lucklow?"

Behind them, a gruff male voice called out. "We don't allow solicitations in this neighborhood."

Journey and Lucas exchanged confused glances before turning around.

An old man dressed in a worn, knotty cardigan, with white hair and a mustache to match, came shuffling up the driveway.

Short and hunched, he was like a gnome out of a children's fairy tale, with a deep frown etched onto his face. He flapped his hands as he reached the stoop in an attempt to shoo them away. "Leave your pamphlets and go."

Journey suppressed a snicker. This wasn't the first time she had been mistaken for a missionary.

"Sir, I'm Special Agent Journey Russo, FBI." She pulled out her badge to show it to the old man, holding it close so his old eyes didn't need to strain. "And this is Special Agent Sullivan. Do you live here with Mr. Lucklow?"

The man recoiled, looking genuinely surprised by the mention of the homeowner's name. Or maybe it was from the suggestion that he lived with another man? "Yes, sir... ma'am. I mean, no, I don't live here."

Why was he so nervous? Did he know something, or was it just his normal reaction to having the FBI show up at his neighbor's door?

"You don't live here?"

He straightened his shoulders. "I'm Samuel Muntz. I live across the street. And I can assure you, we're not looking for trouble around here. Good people live on this block."

If this guy was alert enough to shoo away solicitors as quickly as he'd rushed them, he likely knew a lot about the day-to-day comings and goings of his neighbor.

Self-appointed neighborhood-watch types brought up conflicting emotions within Journey. On the one hand, she hated busybodies who couldn't leave well enough alone. But where Journey and Lucas were concerned, they more often than not were an excellent resource to tap into. Almost as good as all those new video camera doorbells, nosy neighbors made it their business to witness the ins and outs of what was happening in their neighborhoods.

But could she trust this old guy? "When was the last time you recall seeing Mr. Lucklow?"

"Almost forty-eight hours ago." Samuel's response was immediate. "He drove off Thursday as I was eating lunch and hasn't been back since. Police came by yesterday, but he was already gone." The old man's eyes narrowed. "He in trouble?"

"Hopefully not." Journey pulled a business card from her pocket and handed it to him. "Are you certain about the time of Mr. Lucklow's departure, Mr. Muntz?"

"Sure am." Samuel took her card with a curt nod. "I can monitor everything from my front window. I make it my job to know what happens around here. Being retired gives me more time than my working neighbors, so I consider it my duty."

Lucas had moved farther from the house and was examining the home's layout more closely. "What if he pulled into the garage after you went to bed?"

"Nothing gets past me." Conviction hardened Samuel's voice. "He has a terrible garage door opener." His gaze drifted to the empty driveway. "Squeaks loud enough to wake the dead."

Journey and Lucas exchanged glances. If she was reading her partner's expression correctly, they both thought this guy was just nosy enough to be right about Erick Lucklow being gone.

"Have you noticed anything suspicious in the neighborhood?" Journey figured just about anything unusual would stand out in a place as quiet as this.

Samuel shrugged. "Damn kids down the street were skateboarding after dark, and this one time, a car parked at the curb." He growled low in his throat. "Why people think they have to spend every single second of their day staring into a phone, I'll never understand." He wagged a finger at them. "Don't get me started on social med—"

"Would you call us if you see Mr. Lucklow?" Lucas pointed toward the pocket of Samuel's cardigan, where the old man had stuffed Journey's card. He pulled out his own card and offered it as well. "Or you can give him this and ask him to call us."

"Will do." Samuel Muntz tucked the second business card into the same pocket.

"Keep your eyes peeled, just in case, Mr. Muntz." Lucas shook the older man's hand. "Alert us if you see anything suspicious or spot Mr. Lucklow returning home."

Samuel puffed out his chest, and Journey almost expected him to salute. "I'll keep my eyes out. I always do." After a pivot that would have made a general proud, he shuffled back down the driveway.

As they both trudged back toward their car, Journey kept watch to make sure he crossed the street okay, and she noted he was heading toward a redbrick, Craftsman style with a tidy front garden.

She started the car and glanced in her rearview mirror. One last check to watch Lucklow's old neighbor hobble into his home before she pulled away from the curb. "I didn't want to make a decision on our next move under the watchful eye of Captain Cardigan back there."

Lucas snorted. "If every block had a neighbor like that, we'd be out of a job."

"Maybe." Journey snickered. "We'd be better informed. That's for sure. But nosy neighbors don't seem to care about the why as much as the what."

"How so?"

"He knew when Erick Lucklow left and how long it had been." Journey tapped a thumb on the steering wheel, not pulling away just yet. "But Erick is a teacher, and he was last seen here on Thursday. If he came home and left again in the middle of a school day…that's pretty odd."

"Good point. Seems just a bit too convenient, given the circumstances." Lucas nodded. "I'll call the school. Confirm the absence and see if they'll offer any information about it."

"Do we dare to hope he's at a teacher development conference?" Journey reached for her ace of diamonds pendant and rubbed it for luck.

She didn't want to consider the alternative.

24

I'd been waiting for Erick Lucklow to return, monitoring his house from the neighbor's security camera I'd hacked into two days earlier. It was almost too easy, especially after I'd cracked Faulkner's security system.

Technology was an asset to me, breaching people's personal space as simple as breathing. As much as it frustrated me that people were so careless with their private information, I was grateful for their ignorance. Their stupidity was my gain. I had a live feed of Lucklow's front door.

The only issue was waiting. I didn't have enough patience for such a slow process.

There were so many things I needed to do. I couldn't sit here watching a video feed all day. My fingers raced across the keyboard. With a few snippets of code, I set up a trigger to alert me when anyone crossed the camera's field of vision. That freed up my time for more important research.

Lucklow had left his house shortly after the nosy neighbor chased me away. He didn't return to school, and as far as I could tell from the video feed, he hadn't gone back home either.

Where the fuck are you?

I entered a few commands into the terminal and gained remote access through a back door into the school's network. A few more keystrokes, and I had access to Lucklow's emails. There was one to the principal before taking off Thursday afternoon. Sick leave. Planned to be gone the rest of the week.

Sounds to me like he's making a run for it.

No way had Lucklow figured out my mission. That was ludicrous. I'd been so careful, planning out every step…

How did he figure out I'm coming for him?

As I read the email, an alert pinged on my phone. Something had triggered the camera watching Lucklow's home. I pulled up the video feed.

Feds. I recognized them as soon as they appeared on the screen. Despite the distant footage, there was no mistaking the arrogant flip and show of a badge.

What were the Feds doing at Lucklow's? They were talking to that neighbor who'd chased me away. Had they caught on to me? No. That was impossible. I'd worn gloves, wiped away any traces of my blood and prints. I'd even bleached the knife Norman Perry cut me with.

Erick connecting the dots was one thing. The Feds shouldn't have had a clue.

But what if the old guy rats on me?

Panic raced through my veins, speeding my heart.

The old man didn't even give me a chance. He shooed me off the minute I parked. I wasn't there long enough to have even gotten a good look at the shrubs, let alone Lucklow's house.

I watched the old dude flapping his arms as he spoke with

the two agents. He swayed as if struggling to stay upright and hobbled as he walked away.

He's probably senile. The nosy old bastard.

Even if he did still have a few marbles left rattling around in that head of his, cataracts filled those old eyes. He might have seen the color of my car, but there was no way he got or could remember my license plate number. My anonymity was still in place.

Just as that pep talk calmed me down, another worry wormed its way into my mind.

If the Feds are looking for Erick Lucklow, for whatever reason, their investigation is going to screw up my plans.

"I can't bring him justice inside his home. Not with Feds snooping around."

And, well, if he wasn't there…

Where are you?

"You need to improvise." Mother's stern voice pulled my attention away from the screen.

"You don't think they've discovered me, do you?" I didn't like the slight tremble in my voice.

"They're nowhere close to you, my boy." Her blond waves swayed as she shook her head. "Probably after Erick Lucklow for some other crime he's committed. All the more reason for you to bring swift justice."

"Right. But I can't take him out at his house. That screws everything up too."

"Then you'll just have to find another place." She patted my cheek. "You're a smart boy. Hunt him down."

"I can't go chasing after Lucklow like a crazy man either. That's what nearly got me into trouble before. I followed him home. Stupid. And now that old bastard neighbor of his spotted my car. He might ID me if I try to go back there. At the very least, he could raise an alert that a stranger was in the neighborhood, and the Feds could gather all the doorbell footage and..."

Fear kicked me in the stomach. A sick feeling swept over me.

"I need to be patient. Wait until Lucklow lets his guard down again." Looking back at the screen, I pretended to study the unfolding scene, even though I wasn't so much looking at the Feds. "Humans are creatures of habit. I'll track his normal movements for a while. He'll pop up somewhere."

I cursed myself for not putting a tracker on his car. Why would I, though? I'd been so sure of the whens and wheres that it never occurred to me that he'd vanish.

"You have a job to finish." Mother's voice came out low and menacing.

"Don't you think I know that?" I slammed my fists on the desk, anger bubbling up within. My vision blurring, I leaned into my work, my eyes struggling to focus on the miniature figures on the screen before me. "Don't you see what I've accomplished? I can watch everything from right here. He won't come home until he feels safe. There's nothing for me to do until he returns. Then I can track him."

"Not with that nosy neighbor watching the street like a hawk." Mother *tsk*ed. "You need to make a new plan."

"What if I sneak in through the back once I know Lucklow's there?"

The Feds on my screen made a move for their car, and the motion grabbed my attention.

"How is that different than your original plan? If you say going to his house is now an issue, then the back door or front door doesn't matter."

"Well, how else am I going to get him alone?" I detested the whine creeping into my tone.

"You have a destiny to fulfill. And you can't do that while

watching a screen like a little boy in front of his Saturday-morning cartoons."

I slammed my fist on the desk again in frustration. The jolt of pain barely registered against the sting of her insult. "I'll get it done. I just need to figure out another way."

Mother leaned in, her voice in my ear. "Actions speak louder than words."

As soon as she left me alone with my thoughts, shame flooded my cheeks.

Dammit.

Damn her.

Dammit all.

I knew what had to be done. I had to move up my timeline and track him with more precision. I could take him out anywhere as long as I got him alone.

The threat of the Feds lurking around unnerved me, but Mother was right. I had to finish the job. Sooner rather than later.

With trembling hands, I opened a new window on the screen and started piecing together the puzzle of tracking Lucklow's phone.

"I'll show you, Mother. Erick Lucklow will be dead before the day is done."

25

Erick Lucklow stood at a bank of windows, looking out onto an open field just beginning to green. He held a mug of coffee, even though it would be time for dinner soon. Still, the caffeine felt necessary, a preemptive defense against whatever the boogeyman had in store for him.

He'd be ready, come what may.

Glancing around at his surroundings, serene and humble, with neither a friend nor foe in sight, he was almost tempted to laugh. He'd called his brother in a panic from his vehicle on Thursday as he was leaving his house to go where no one could find him.

"What's going on, Erick? Pull over. You sound too manic to be driving." His brother was three years older but decades more successful. Daniel owned his own financial services firm, with a portfolio of rich clients. He had a closet full of tailored suits and owned three houses.

Erick, a schoolteacher, looked like a pauper compared to Dan. But money never came between them. Dan was a big brother in good times and bad. No matter what Erick told him he needed, insane or not, Dan stepped up to help.

Not wanting to risk telling his brother the truth, he gave Dan a story about being burned out and just needing to get away for a few days to clear his head. Dan didn't know what had happened on that hunting trip, and Erick could never tell him.

Without a second thought, Dan offered his vacation cabin out by Cheat Lake in West Virginia, promising to keep his location a secret so no one would bother him while he took some time to relax in nature.

When Dan bought the old A-frame house five years earlier, it had been a dump. A forgotten structure on a piece of neglected land. The location was perfect. Lake views, access to the marina, and enough trees surrounding it to feel isolated from the rest of the world. And all that while being just an hour south of Pittsburgh. Erick, his brother, and his sister-in-law envisioned turning the place into a weekend getaway for the whole family to use.

The first year Erick and Dan spent every weekend out there, knocking out walls and refinishing floors. The house wasn't large, but it was grand in its own way, and Erick found the cozy building peaceful.

I'm good. He took a deep breath. *Totally fine.* That made the hundredth time he'd reminded himself.

Erick stood, watching rain drizzle outside. He'd been there for more than a day without incident and could stay as long as he liked. There was plenty of firewood, booze, and a simmering pot of chili waiting to be devoured.

He checked his watch. Almost five. Not quite whiskey o'clock, but close enough. Flipping on the kitchen lights and pulling a bottle from the cabinet, he poured himself a drink and took a long swallow.

That was when glass shattered. The sound came from the utility room.

What the...? Erick's spine turned to ice. Something, or someone, must have bashed in the utility room window.

The lights in the kitchen and living room went out, and the dull, rainy day turned the rooms instantly gray.

Shit! Shit! Shit!

Erick cowered next to the stove and reached for the gun he'd kept holstered at his hip. But it wasn't there. He'd let his guard down and taken it off, setting it on the coffee table in the living room when he'd gone to use the bathroom.

He cursed himself for being sloppy. Now that he needed a weapon, his Glock mocked him from the other room.

For a moment, he considered darting across the area for it, but the space was too open. Most of the A-frame home was just a giant room with a few counters and pony walls to segregate space.

Once he moved from behind the stove, it would be open season on him.

He took a breath and checked himself. Slowed his heart rate so the pounding in his ears wasn't the only sound he could take in. Catastrophizing wouldn't help. And as he calmed his nerves, Erick realized he'd detected nothing moving since the crash.

Maybe what he'd heard was just a tree branch smashing through the window. And if the wind was blowing hard enough to do that, it was also strong enough to have brought down a power line.

He wished to God in Heaven that were true. Only, he knew it wasn't the wind attacking him. The rain outside was nothing more than a drizzle.

"Who's out there? Announce yourself or be shot!"

Erick watched for movement while his mind scrambled for options. Dashing across the room for his gun was a death wish.

Knives.

He was in a kitchen. There were blades of every shape and size. But they were inside a closed drawer…just out of reach.

Then he remembered the chili.

Slowly, he unbuttoned his flannel shirt and pulled it off. He wrapped one sleeve around his hand, just tight enough so it wouldn't slip, then grabbed the pot of chili by the handle.

Time to eat, boogeyman.

"What are you waiting for?" The confidence of knowing his next move brought a mocking bravado to his voice. "Come out. Last warning."

Erick waited through the silence, his heart thundering as he tried to slow his breathing and listen for the moment to strike.

He was positioned at the only entrance to the kitchen, crouched there next to the stove. Whoever was here would have to come at him from the front. As he adjusted his position, the heat from the pot traveled up the handle and threatened to sear through the flannel into his hand. But he didn't waver. He would burn his flesh to the bone if it meant keeping his life.

The black toe of a boot peeked across the threshold.

Come on, you son of a bitch. One more step.

As soon as the boogeyman stepped into view, Erick lifted the pot, ready to throw its bubbling contents.

The room flashed white with a loud *bang.*

Erick lost his grip as a silent scream of pain clawed up his throat.

Chunky red matter filled the air. Tomatoes, beans, and beef rained from above.

Boiling sauce hit his skin and burned its way down his flesh.

Erick tried to move, but his legs gave out. He slipped to

the floor, landing in a pool of beans covered in a sauce far too red to have come from his chili.

"You thought you hid from me, but it was just sad watching you try."

That voice. He'd heard it before, but Erick couldn't remember where.

The boogeyman continued to mock him as he drew closer. "Turns out, none of you were as smart as you thought you were."

"I didn't kill him." Erick gagged on the spices clogging his sinuses. He coughed and struggled for breath as he pushed the words from his lips. "It…wasn't my fault."

"Maybe not. But that's for you and God to work out." The boogeyman's black boots came into view, smattered with blood and bits of red beans. "After you, there's just one left."

A gentle breeze blew across the back of Erick's neck before a white-hot strike of lightning cracked his skull.

26

Journey and Lucas did a little searching around the web and located Erick's brother. A few phone calls later, they had an address.

As they raced toward West Virginia, Journey dissected the conversation she'd had with Daniel Lucklow. "We're walking into a potential crisis scenario."

"Talk to me." Lucas's eyes were glued to the road as he weaved to pass slower vehicles.

"Daniel's concern about Erick's well-being, for starters. Burnout is real, sure, but would his symptoms be bad enough to make his brother worry he might do something drastic?"

"Burnout can manifest in different ways. Maybe his reaction is symptomatic of a more serious mental health issue?" Lucas tipped his head in a noncommittal nod. "Did the brother say whether Erick had a history of depression? Or maybe someone in their family has mental health issues?"

"Nothing specific." Journey caught the last glimpse of the disappearing Pittsburgh skyline in the rearview mirror. She shook her head. "Just that he was worried. Made him sound like a perfectionist on the verge of a nervous breakdown.

And at the same time, a man who loved his students and would never leave them stranded."

"All right, let's play that out. What would make a dedicated educator leave so suddenly?"

"Daniel said his brother was trying to isolate himself from everything to help him ease the work pressure, but he knew there was something else bothering him." Her brain ticked through several possibilities.

"You think he might be involved? Erick, I mean?" Lucas filled in the silence, saying the one thing Journey didn't want to. "You think he's not the next target but on the other side of the gun? Like he might be our killer?"

It was a definite possibility that Erick might be running from the law. Everyone from that hunting party was involved in some way. But Erick as the killer—that just didn't sit right. Not with the way Daniel had described his brother. Erick was a devoted father and teacher.

"No. I doubt he's involved in the criminal side." Journey considered guilt by association. That, too, felt wrong. "He's running because he's worried he's next. Which might suggest he knows something about the murders."

"But if you need to run, why tell your brother?"

Journey understood exactly why Erick had reached out to Daniel. "I'd do the same with Michelle." She had another thought. "Or maybe he's got something to hide?"

"Fair points. We'll have to proceed with caution. If he's as scared as his brother suggested, we don't want him to think he's backed into a corner when we get there. Badge or not, he might lash out."

"Exactly. Desperate equals unpredictable." Journey had learned that lesson from experience. The first night she'd brought Dracula home from the shelter, the damn cat hid behind her couch and refused to come out. He'd been living on the streets for so long before the shelter took him in, and they'd warned her he'd be skittish. Journey thought she could overcome that easily, but when treats and toys didn't work, she reached her hands into his little hidey-hole to pull the scared cat out.

She'd ended up needing stitches.

Darkness settled heavily overhead as the clouds thickened with every passing mile. Conversation eventually went silent, and by the time they neared the address, the sun had completely hidden behind the blanket of gray.

A wall of pine trees shielded the house from the road as they turned down the long driveway, unsure of what to expect at the other end. They emerged into a large open plot of land surrounded by a meadow and, at its heart, a modest A-frame house with a small outbuilding, or possibly a garage, behind.

The silver 2017 Ford Escape parked by the house was the same car DMV records had listed in Erick Lucklow's name. Journey had looked it up on the way.

She leaned over the dash, examining the scene. It could've been the setting for a Hallmark movie. That is, if she hadn't sensed something foreboding. "I don't love this. We've had our headlights on for the past half hour, but there's not a single light on inside that house."

Lucas killed the engine. "I'll grab flashlights from the trunk in case we need them when we get inside."

"This may have just become a wellness check." The dark house, plus Daniel's concern, heightened her caution instincts. "Put on your vest. I'll cover the rear."

Lucas handed her a flashlight and flicked his chin, silently agreeing. They both donned protective vests before quietly moving toward the house, bypassing the gravel sidewalk for the lawn.

Journey double-timed it around the back, stepping carefully as she went. There was no path along the side of the house, and the wet grass on which she walked was young, just beginning to green. Dead leaves and twigs scattered the surface. It wasn't a well-manicured yard from the suburbs, fertilized and trimmed to perfection, so she moved slowly, stepped softly, keeping a keen eye for anything that looked out of place in the already-messy landscape.

She stealthed past the peaked section of the house, the part that gave an A-frame its name. The other half was a squat utilitarian block, in front of which she now stood. It was tacked onto the side like an architectural afterthought.

Lucas's voice echoed from the gloom. "Erick Lucklow?" He'd waited before knocking, allowing her sufficient lead time to cover the back. "It's Special Agents Russo and Sullivan with the FBI. We'd like to check on you, make sure you're okay."

Journey scanned the exterior wall and cursed under her breath when she noted a flimsy utility door. A jagged hole in the glass greeted her, just above the brass doorknob.

They officially had probable cause to enter.

Lucas knocked again, and Journey shot him an urgent, telepathic message to *shut up*. The utility door was ajar, and her every instinct screamed, *Erick can't answer*.

She turned on the flashlight and nudged the door open with her toe. The utility room was maybe ten feet by ten feet, though the flashlight beam could have skewed her perspective. Straight ahead, a side-by-side washer and dryer stood against a concrete wall. She moved her beam to three o'clock and found a water heater and utility sink. Both corners were clear.

Lucklow must have been in the process of making chili for supper, because even out in the utility room, the air wept with garlic and peppers, cumin, and tomato.

Behind the door, the fuse box cover was open, and a

quick scan of the switches revealed the master switch had been thrown, cutting the power.

Just like at Faulkner's Guns & Ammo and Norman Perry's place.

The odds of finding Erick Lucklow alive sank to a snowball's chance in Hell. If the bastard behind all this killing was still in the house, she'd put him away.

Needing to connect with Lucas before changing tactics, she backed out of the room and into the yard.

He was just turning the corner from the opposite side of the house. "Front's locked—"

She lifted a finger to her lips. Then she pointed her flashlight at the broken window and motioned for him to follow her back inside.

Her beam led them to the fuse box. With luck, reengaging the master switch would flood the house with light. She pulled a glove from her jacket pocket and put it on.

Lucas raised three fingers and counted her down—*three, two, one.*

Journey flipped the master switch back to the on position. The living room and kitchen appeared under the light of two small fixtures. Helpful but hardly intimidating.

How long ago was the fuse switched off, if so few lights were on when the power was killed?

Journey motioned toward the interior of the main house. Lucas moved left, and she took the right side, stepping from the utility room to the open, vaulted body of the main living area.

The pungent odor of garlic was stronger now. Journey's nostrils burned from the cloying spices floating in the air, but there was something else, too, a sour smell that didn't mix well with the others. She couldn't name the scent that made her want to hold her breath, but instinct told her it wasn't a good sign.

Picture windows along the back looked out onto a field of grass. Lucas passed by quickly, clearing the rear corners as he went, as if careful to avoid making himself a target for a bullet through the glass.

Journey began clearing the right side of the room on her way to the kitchen.

No one was behind the couch or oversize club chairs. No one in the closet. Only the kitchen remained unsecured.

Seconds later, Journey turned the corner formed by the stove and counters, her flashlight beam finding what she'd been smelling. Remnants of a ruined pot of chili were splattered on the wall, across the counter, and mingled with a viscous, deep-red pool on the floor surrounding Erick Lucklow's lifeless body. His eyes stared blankly at the ceiling, and flies had already begun to swarm around his facial wounds.

Her throat constricted. "Body."

Lucas, just a few feet away, turned an ear toward her, his gaze still roving the area. "What?"

"Body!" Defeat brought her almost to her knees until anger sprang her back upright. "Over here."

Lucas moved to the kitchen and crouched beside the corpse, taking in the ruined pot of food splattered on the wall and across the counter, mixing with all the blood. He shook his head gravely. "Erick Lucklow?"

Journey nodded and stooped to press her fingers to his throat. No pulse, but he was still warm.

"Is that chili?"

"Hard to tell where Lucklow's dinner ends and his blood begins." Journey turned away from the body. "Better call this in."

The local sheriff's department was quick to dispatch a few cars, saying they had more on the way. Journey and Lucas stood outside while local officers secured the crime scene. Flashes from cameras illuminated the darkness as evidence markers were laid out all around the house.

Michelle and the rest of the forensic team were on their way. Sirens already wailed in the distance as Journey spotted a shadow dashing behind the garage.

"Did you see that?" Acting on instinct, she called out. "Hey you, stop!"

When she threw herself forward, her leather shoes slipped against the rain-slick grass.

Journey stumbled, and by the time she'd righted herself, Lucas was fifteen yards ahead, running full steam across the lawn toward a man headed for the pine trees and, beyond that, the road. Rather than try to catch up, Journey zagged left for the driveway, positioned to intercept if the guy changed course.

Lucas's voice thundered through the cold. "FBI. Stop right there!"

Gravel crunched underfoot as Journey made it to the road just in time to see the runner throwing himself into a dinged-up white Toyota Corolla.

27

I slammed my foot against the accelerator, the car's engine roaring. The white lines of the highway seemed to blur together and become one long, winding pathway that whipped past my window. Terror bubbled up inside as I glanced at the speedometer. It hovered around eighty miles an hour.

I'd seen those same Feds snooping around Erick's home back in Pittsburgh. I should've expected them to figure out he'd gone into hiding. He hadn't really been all that hard for me to track down. At least I got to him before they did.

Still, that was too close of a call. I'd barely finished with Erick and made it back to my car before they pulled down the driveway.

I thought I'd gotten away without being seen, but one thing was clear. They were catching on much faster than I'd expected. Too fast. My pulse raced as that thought wormed its way through my mind.

But how is that possible? They couldn't have connected each of the men. Could they?

If I wanted to finish my task, I'd have to hurry.

Blue and red lights flashed as police cars raced down the opposite side of the highway, headed toward the cabin. It wouldn't be long before law enforcement had every road covered with officers on alert.

I had to slow down. I needed to breathe.

My hands were like lead weights on the steering wheel as I willed myself to take the off-ramp to the access road. I turned toward a small strip mall and could just make out the lights of a fast-food burger joint in the dark. It seemed like a good place to cool off and get my head straight.

As I turned into the darkened parking lot, a patrol car pulled out of the drive-through lane and immediately flipped on its siren. Red and blue flooded my vision.

My heart seized.

I screamed out for Mother, even though I knew she wouldn't answer.

My hands, slick with sweat, slipped from the wheel as my foot slammed on the brake. "Holy freakin' crap."

The police cruiser sped by and tore down the highway to join the others, which had passed me only moments earlier.

A hot tear dripped down the length of my cheek. "I'm not crying. I'm not a pussy. It's just shock, that's all." I eased the car into a parking spot and killed the engine.

I was glad Mother hadn't been there, but she was always listening. I sensed the bitterness of her judgment in the back of my throat. My gut cramped and twisted in the silence. I popped the cover on the center console, looking for a napkin or tissue to wipe away the shame.

That was when I saw it. The gun splattered in red and in plain view on the passenger's seat. I thanked my lucky stars I'd made it this far without getting caught. How could I have been so stupid as to leave it sitting there while driving so recklessly? A speeding ticket would've spelled my doom.

"Get rid of it." The night was unraveling. I was acting

sloppy. I had to get myself back under control. "Wipe it down. Throw it in the dumpster and move on."

I scavenged through the back seat for a cloth, scrubbed the gun off as best as I could manage, and tossed it in the garbage with the rest of the trash from the greasy burger joint.

With the cruise control set at exactly sixty-five, I relaxed just enough to strategize my next set of moves. Somehow, those Feds were connecting the murders. I should've realized something was up when I saw them snooping around Erick's place.

Mother wanted me to hurry, but I knew that wasn't the smartest play. She urged me to bring swift justice, but in all that rushing around, I'd overlooked something. How were those federal agents putting it all together? I'd been so careful, disposing of the weapons and making each death look like a random robbery. How, how, *how*?

Maybe they *hadn't* figured it out.

What if the Feds snooping around Lucklow's place were just an unlucky coincidence?

Mother had said as much. Erick Lucklow was, after all, guilty.

I wouldn't have been there to bring justice to him if he were an innocent, law-abiding, God-fearing man. Maybe Mother had been right, and they were after him for their own reasons.

I could speculate on that until the sun came up and never know the truth. The fact was, I still had one last name to check off my list to complete my mission. And I couldn't let the Feds get there before me.

For all I knew, they might already be safeguarding the area.

That would make for a real annoyance but not an impossible challenge.

A hunter who knew their prey would eventually make the kill. The key to success was knowing their desires and weaknesses.

An empty stomach would drive a bear out of its den. It just took the right bait to lure it from safety.

For Faulkner, it was hubris. The man had grown vain and overconfident in the gun shop. The empire he'd built. He believed he was the most secure and untouchable man in the world. It was such a satisfying irony to point out how he'd been surrounded by weapons that did nothing to protect him in his final moments.

Perry…the rich bastard. So concerned with having it all. He'd gotten the big house, fancy car, expensive toys, and gadgets. He claimed it was for his family, but they'd abandoned him. Once I took away the power, his expensive gadgets couldn't save him. And all alone, there was no one there to hear his final pitiful cries as he bled to death in the basement.

Then there was Lucklow, the frightened little rat. So desperate to stay safe. It'd been almost too easy to figure out where he'd run off to. A little boy darting into his big brother's room because he was too scared to sleep alone. It was pitiful watching a grown man behave like that. So predictable and sad.

But what of my next and final victim? What desires and weaknesses could I exploit?

Family was always a good pressure point. Spouses were an easy target. And then I remembered Melinda.

The daughter. Oh, yes. How could she have slipped my mind? All grown up now and all the more fun to play with.

I took the next exit. Stopped. Pulled out my phone. Googled her. Mapped the address.

God, it really was almost too easy.

Time to go round up my bait.

28

"Hands where we can see them!" Lucas had his service weapon ready as he advanced on the dinged-up white Toyota Corolla from the front.

Journey flanked him and assumed a tactical position, looking at him for further instructions.

Behind the windshield, hands rose in compliance with his order.

"Step out of the vehicle." Lucas held his stance, keen for any sudden movement. "Nice and slow. Keep those hands where we can see them."

A young man emerged from behind the wheel, both hands raised high above his head in surrender. He barely looked old enough to drive, his baby face framed with soft waves of brown hair.

His voice broke like a pubescent teenager's. "Please don't shoot me!"

Journey rushed toward the kid and grabbed his arm. She spun him around and pushed his body up against the car, securing his wrists with handcuffs.

Lucas holstered his gun and closed in. "What were you doing here, and why did you run?"

The kid smelled strongly of hot dogs and stale coffee.

"I'm a true crime podcaster." He whimpered as the cuffs clicked home. "I just got off work and saw all the crazy with police sirens screaming past me. I thought it could be great material for my show. That's all. I swear."

Journey patted down his torso and retrieved his wallet from his pocket. "Trevor Mason, about to celebrate his twenty-first birthday."

A little snot dribbled from Mason's nose where he had his face pressed against the car. He sniffled. "I keep recording equipment in the trunk in case something like this ever happens. Even though it never does. Except for tonight. I promise. I didn't touch anything. I was just there trying to capture something cool I could broadcast."

Lucas noticed the *Kwiki Gas* logo printed on Trevor's shirt pocket. "You said you were just leaving work. Is this your uniform?"

"I'm a cashier." Trevor's voice cracked as if he might cry. "You can call my supervisor. I just got off work at six thirty. They have cameras on me all night. You can confirm it. Please. You've got to believe me."

Lucas glanced out of the corner of his eye at Trevor's car and then stared off in the direction of Erick's house. "We need a safe place to hold the kid so we can check out his story."

"Get my phone. Call anyone in my contacts. They'll tell you about my job. I hate it. And my podcast. It's called *Case Confidential*." Trevor's eyes watered, his breath hitching as he continued to babble. "I didn't have nothing to do with whatever happened at that house. I swear. You gotta believe me."

Journey nodded toward the police vehicles parked

around the crime scene. "Let's stick him in the back of a squad car while we check out his story."

"Yes. Please. Check me out. I'll do whatever you need." Trevor eagerly complied with every instruction, folding his lanky frame into the cramped back seat.

A short time later, Trevor Mason's information was confirmed. He had been at work until a full hour after Lucas and Journey arrived on scene. The kid couldn't have had anything to do with what happened to Erick Lucklow.

But to Lucas, Trevor wasn't just an innocent bystander. "True crime isn't entertainment. You may think you were just trying to get some good content for your followers, but real people's lives are at stake here. You want to make a contribution to your community? Submit any footage captured tonight for review. That's where it will do some real good."

Trevor tearfully agreed. He was jelly by the time they finished their chat, and Lucas left Trevor in the hands of the sheriff and Journey as he went to greet Michelle. She was the first member of the FBI forensic team to arrive.

He walked her around to the back of the house, where the broken utility door had been the point of entry for the perp. "Did Journey warn you?" He watched her pull a pair of latex gloves over her fingers.

"About what?" Michelle flexed her hands inside the gloves, her expression eager and curious.

"The chili." He grinned. "It's pretty spicy in there."

Gallows humor was a fairly normal coping strategy in this line of work, even though it wasn't for everyone.

"Ooh. Red or white?" Michelle met his gaze with an eager expression. "Ever had it Cincinnati style? It's surprisingly good."

Not the reaction Lucas expected. He didn't know her well enough to judge whether she was screwing with him or if she seriously didn't know what she was about to walk into.

"After what I saw in there, I don't think I'll be eating any chili style for a long time."

"Don't knock it until you try it." Michelle rolled her eyes playfully. "Now, let's go find out which kind is covering that body."

Lucas's jaw dropped. Had he actually heard those words come out of her mouth? Even more concerning was wondering whether he should be amused or concerned by Michelle's dark joke.

"You okay?" Michelle's expression shifted. "You're not going to be sick on me, are you?"

"No. I'm good." He shook his head, not wanting to appear unprofessional. "Is your team all here?"

"They were right behind me on the highway." Michelle looked back toward the road as a pair of headlights appeared. "There they are now. Let's go ahead and get started. Walk me around the scene."

"Let's start here." Lucas motioned to the utility room door. "This is where we entered. Journey found the glass broken and the door ajar."

Michelle stepped closer, then jotted a note on her clipboard before placing a tag. "Perfect place for a window if you're trying to give a burglar easy access to the doorknob." Four small panes in the middle of the aluminum door formed an eye-level square. "Did you find an object that may have been used to break it?"

"Nothing. Could've used an elbow." Lucas lined his elbow up with the glass, mimicking the motion. The hole looked about the size of a large fist, and he examined the shards that remained in the pane for fibers. "Actually, I'd put money on it being a rock...the one he used to bash Lucklow's head in. Once the glass was compromised, all the intruder needed to do was reach through and twist the dead bolt."

Michelle jotted a note. "Did you touch the knob when you entered the home? We need to dust for fingerprints, and knowing who all touched it helps. Check the glass for DNA or other residues."

"No. Agent Russo said the door was cracked open, and she nudged it open with her shoe. The handle wasn't contaminated by either of us."

They walked through the rest of the small room and traced the path he and Journey took into the house. Lucas explained that he'd cleared the bedroom while Journey headed to the kitchen.

Michelle thanked him for the overview, then excused herself as she directed members of her team.

Lucas stood there for a moment, watching them get to work dusting, examining, and bagging. Then he turned his attention to the M.E.

The man stood front-loaded, a heavy belly hanging from his torso as if pointing the way for the rest of him. His black mustache danced on his lip as he introduced himself. "Art Morgen." The M.E. waved a gloved palm instead of giving a handshake.

Lucas stifled a laugh. "Your name is *Morg*-en? Seems a little on the nose for a medical examiner."

He shrugged with the nonchalance only a man who'd heard all the jokes could possess. "It was either that or become a painter."

Dr. Morgen paused for the laugh, but Lucas didn't get the joke.

"My first name's Art."

"Ah!" At least Lucas's weren't the only poor attempts at humor anymore. "Well, Dr. Morgen, what can you tell me so far?"

"Considering I only just walked into the room..." He groaned. "The only thing I can tell you so far is that I wish this guy had been making white chili instead."

Every bit of splatter was going to require analysis.

"There are a few things to note, though." He knelt and motioned for Lucas to follow. "Victim has a single gunshot wound here." He pointed to Lucklow's belly, where a near-black swell of blood soaked the front of his flannel shirt. "Also, contusion above the right temple, here." Again, he pointed. "Definite head trauma. See how the eyeball appears abnormally recessed?"

Lucas would have to take Morgen's word for it. Lucklow's face was purple with swelling and red with splatter, nothing close to human. "So the blow to the head was fatal?"

"This is a pretty nasty blow. Depending on the impact on the brain, it can cause bleeding, sometimes cerebral edema or swelling. But I won't know for sure until I get a peek under the hood."

The good doctor knew how to keep a dark moment light. "What else?"

"Contact burns on his face and hands. My best guess at this point, judging from the pattern and location, is that it's from the chili. Tomatoes are highly acidic. Couple acid with temperatures near or above boiling, and burns intensify." He pointed to a circle of angry blisters around Lucklow's eyes. "My initial thinking, judging from the direction of the splash-back on his face, is that he may have tried to use the pot of chili in self-defense. But he was shot before he could launch it and flailed his arm instead, dumping everything on himself."

"Think the perp got hit by the chili too?"

Morgen shrugged. "I'll need more time to examine the splash pattern, but if he did, look for burns. Reddening of the skin mostly. But the delicate skin around the eyes and lips would likely blister wherever the chili hit it."

Michelle approached, holding an evidence bag up for Lucas to see. It contained a single shell casing. "Found right over there." She pointed to a circle on the floor in the kitchen's corner, where the photographer was just wrapping up.

The casing had been lying only about three feet away from Lucklow's body under the lower kitchen cabinets. Lucas wasn't surprised that both he and Journey had overlooked it during their precursory examination of the scene.

He held the evidence bag at eye level, directly addressing the small piece of metal. "Let's hope you help break this case."

29

Journey drove back to the FBI Pittsburgh Field Office like a woman on a mission, making it back from the crime scene in West Virginia in just under an hour. The Bureau Ford squealed around the corners of the garage as Journey slammed on the brakes and swung tight into an empty parking space. She didn't need to turn her head to see Lucas glaring at her from the passenger seat, so she pretended she didn't notice.

"Thanks for not killing us. I've never wanted any of my fellow agents to have to peel my face off a cement pillar."

"At least they'd have to say we died in the line of duty." She smirked as she checked the time. It was almost nine. The night had been a hell of a roller coaster, and they weren't finished yet. "C'mon. Clock's ticking."

As soon as they reached the bullpen, Journey made a straight line for the murder board. She grabbed the sticky notes and added a third column for Erick Lucklow.

"Hey." Lucas picked up a folder from the desk and waved it at her. "Looks like the National Park Service case file on Jerry Minton was finally sent over while we were out." He flipped through it. "Nine-one-one transcripts. Witness interviews for each of the four guys. And an autopsy report."

"Ooh." Journey held out her hand. "Let me see." It didn't take long to confirm her suspicion. "Wouldn't you know? Jerry Minton wasn't just shot. He suffered a head injury too. That makes four men shot in the gut as well as struck on the head."

"Technically five, if you count Noah Hudson, the park ranger. Our first unsolved murder victim."

She set the file down between her and Lucas. "Anyway. My point is, the injuries appear consistent. Four hunting buddies, four nearly identical blows to the head."

Lucas grabbed the file and flipped through the pages. "And guess who took statements the night it all happened?" He turned the file out so Journey could read the name.

She didn't even need to look. "Noah Hudson." She smiled as all the dots connected. "He was the ranger on duty that night. He took their statements."

"Five people connected to that hunting trip." Lucas held his hand up and wiggled his fingers to emphasize his point. "With five nearly identical wounds."

"It's all connecting now." Journey turned to look at the names on the board. "If we can get to the last hunter in that party, we might be able to stop the killer in his tracks."

"We'd better get on the road and go find Rob Larson."

Journey glanced at her phone, checking the time. "It's so late."

"I know. But we can't risk waiting until morning." Lucas flipped the folder open again. "I'll double-check the address listed for him."

Moments later, they sprinted back to the car and headed for a neighborhood fifteen minutes west of their office. Lucas took the wheel. Journey grabbed the sheriff's report. "I'll read while you drive."

Digging more deeply into the file on the original NPS case, Journey came upon a lengthy description of the victim, Jerry Minton. "He was only forty-two when he died. He left behind a sixteen-year-old son named Corey." She thumbed the pages inside the folder. The Minton family lived near the Faulkners until just after the hunting incident. "Corey Minton was sent to live with grandparents."

Lucas glanced over at her. "Where was the mother?"

Near the bottom, she found an asterisk, which she summarized aloud. "Caroline Minton died two years prior to the accident. Ovarian cancer."

On the back was stapled a family photo on which someone had written the subjects' names and ages. *Jerry, 40. Caroline, 39. Corey, 14.* She clicked on her phone's flashlight and leaned in for a better look. Caroline was already showing signs of her fate, her skin sallow and thin. Jerry stood behind her with a stoic expression and a hand resting on Caroline's shoulder. Corey barely registered a smile.

Poor kid must have known he was about to lose his mother.

Then Journey spotted something about him that looked familiar. "Pull over."

Lucas grunted. "Easier said than done." They were on the interstate, but he didn't argue and took the next exit. He found an empty parking lot and stopped.

She handed him the family photo. "What do you see?"

"Who is this?"

She didn't want to say, didn't want to influence his thinking, but he'd already spotted the names and ages. "Jerry and his wife and son."

"I thought you said she died before the hunting accident."

"The picture was taken two years before the shooting. Keep looking."

Instead, he turned his attention to her. "I'm tired, and I'm trying to preserve my energy for the night ahead. Give me more, please."

That was fair. "If I've done the math right, Jerry's son, Corey, would be twenty-three now. He's fourteen in that photo."

"Okay?"

"Age his appearance."

Lucas nodded and studied the kid's face. "Not a lot to go on. He's sort of got a boy-next-door look here. Except for the fact you can see he knows his mom is dying. I remember that age, and it was hard enough without having to contend with cancer and death."

"Look at his hairline." She leaned over and pointed to the spot that had grabbed her attention. "That cowlick."

He held the image closer to the light. Then nodded, seeing it. "The police sketch. What we thought might just be a bad haircut." He dropped his head onto the headrest and rubbed his eyes. "Are we looking at a kid who grew up and took vengeance on his dad's hunting buddies?"

"Maybe." Journey retrieved the image and stared at it again. "Granted, it's a long shot. This was taken nine years ago. And we're comparing it to an eyewitness sketch."

Eyewitness descriptions were the bad joke of investigative work. Couldn't live with 'em, couldn't live without 'em. Countless studies had proved that a brain under distress could be notoriously inaccurate.

Witnesses gave suspects tattoos they didn't have and accents they didn't speak with. A white man with black hair might be described as Asian. A pregnant woman might be disabled and fat. All discrepancies were the unintentional result of a manic mind desperately trying to make sense of stimuli it had never been asked to interpret before.

And yet investigators needed to know what they were

looking for, so a partially inaccurate description was better than no description at all. At least, most of the time.

Journey pulled out her phone and entered Jerry Minton's details into the public records database. That gave her Corey's birth certificate and date of birth, which led her to his social security number and last known address. If only every search were that easy.

"He lives in San Clemente, California."

At that, Lucas perked up. "I think I've got an old navy buddy who went to work for the San Clemente Police Department when he got out." He scrolled through his phone to find his friend's number and texted him.

His phone rang within seconds.

"Ramon. How's it going, man? Thanks for getting back to me so quick."

Journey couldn't help but marvel at the network of law enforcement buddies spread across the country, from small towns to major cities, each willing to serve as a candle in an investigative storm.

"Thanks. I owe you a beer next time I'm in town." He hung up, a fat smile filling his face. "They're sending a patrol officer to Corey's house to see if he's home and willing to answer a few questions."

"You're a wizard."

He chuckled. "At least for the next five minutes."

They took a collective breath. They'd accomplished something, taken action, and regardless of what they might find, that deserved at least a second of recognition.

"All right." Lucas put the car back in drive. "Let's go find Rob Larson."

30

Journey and Lucas arrived at Rob Larson's redbrick rambler just after nine thirty and found the porch illuminated by a single light bulb. She knocked and stepped back to wait with Lucas on the front porch. The hour was late, and Journey imagined the negative reception they were about to receive.

After her first knock went unanswered, she was about to give it another try when the door creaked open.

In the doorway stood a man whose grizzled beard hadn't been trimmed in weeks, and his rumpled flannel had definitely seen better days. He leaned heavily against the doorframe as a prop to stand upright. Before either of them could introduce themselves, he blurted out, "You came. I thought I was going to my grave with all these secrets."

When a man opened his door and his first instinct was to blurt out what sounded like a confession, a special agent's instincts went into overdrive. Journey scanned him for weapons and checked the space around him for other threats.

The only observation of note was that he had to rely on

the doorframe to remain standing. She sniffed, expecting alcohol, but detected none.

"I'm going to ask you to take a step back, sir," Journey said calmly.

"Okay." He stumbled on a discarded shoe behind him and ended up on his knees. "I'm sorry."

Lucas's hand moved slowly to his hip, his eyes locked on Larson.

Journey looked past the entryway, trying to judge the scene. Just beyond where they stood lay the family room, the dim light tinged with flashes of color from a soundless TV. Empty soda cans lay atop dirty plates on the cluttered coffee table. A laptop sat open on the couch.

She listened for movement. Watched for shadows. Nothing.

"I'm Special Agent Journey Russo, FBI." She flashed her badge while introducing Lucas, her eyes continuing to scan. "Are you Robert Larson?"

He nodded, still on his knees, looking up at them but not trying to stand. "I go by Rob."

Journey visually inspected his clothing and hands, looking for blood.

Lucas leaned in for a closer examination of his face. "Are you here alone, Mr. Larson?"

"Unfortunately, yeah." He scoffed. "My wife and I are separated, and our daughter has her own apartment. I've been here all night. On Facebook." He pointed in the vague direction of the couch. "My laptop is there. You can see for yourself."

Hearing him speak clearly and in complete sentences made Journey's adrenaline drop a notch. She was still on alert but no longer piqued. Larson was compliant, answering their questions and doing as asked. He didn't make any unexpected moves.

She needed more info. "Mr. Larson, you're visibly upset, and when you opened the door, your introduction suggested you were expecting someone. Why is that?"

"Police came by a couple days after Sam was murdered." He groaned, the sound suddenly sticky with fear. "I didn't answer. Too scared. Then I saw Norman's name in the obituaries."

Lucas twitched, ready to move if necessary. "Why were you scared of speaking to the officers?"

"It's the curse. Sam Faulkner and Norman Perry." Emotion strangled his voice as he held up a finger for each name. "We were on a hunting trip together. Something terrible happened. And it's coming for me."

Journey caught Lucas's eye, trying to read his mind. They'd come to chat with Larson as the last survivor and stumbled across a broken man. She examined his hands and tried to get a look at his fingernails. The light was dim, but to her discerning eye, they were free of visible traces of blood.

No signs of chili burns on his face or hands. His flannel shirt exuded an aroma, but it was flecked with more than just his last few meals. Bits of paint dotted the fibers, evidencing the sort of work shirt every homeowner kept at the back of the closet for odd jobs.

"Can you tell us why you said you were waiting for someone?"

Larson laughed. The sort of chuckle that said, *What the hell?* "Because of the *math*. There were five of us on that trip, and three are now dead. Lucklow, number four, has vanished online, so I can only assume he's either dead or hiding. Which leaves me. And where am I going to go? I'm broke. Got nothing. I figured the next person who came was going to kill me or save me."

Journey exchanged glances with Lucas. His gaze had quit darting, and his brows no longer pinched out a scowl. "We have some information about Erick Lucklow, and we'd like to ask you a few questions. Are you willing to come with us to the field office? It's best if we speak there."

"Is he dead?" Larson's voice rose with the question, but his face said he already knew the answer.

Lucas offered a hand to help him stand. "Let's get you out of here first."

"Yeah, yeah. I'd like that. I don't feel safe here. But you need to listen." He didn't move, and Lucas's hand hovered empty in the space between them.

Lucas lowered his palm an inch, urging Larson along. "We'll give you all the time you need to say whatever's on your mind. But first, we want to get you someplace safe. Then we can talk."

He paused but accepted Lucas's help and slowly made his way to his feet. "Wait, you're FBI?"

It was nearing ten p.m. when they settled into the fourth-floor conference room nearest to the bullpen. They were too far away for Larson to see the murder board but close enough to show it to him if it came to that.

The fluorescent lighting in the room felt too harsh for this time of night, but at least there was a coffee maker. Small comforts went a long way, especially on late nights like these.

Lucas brewed a fresh pot and poured everyone a cup.

Journey took a sip and shuddered at how bitter and weak it tasted. She smiled appreciatively, choosing not to comment on how much she wished it were as good as the coffee from their new favorite coffee shop. It was the jolt of caffeine she needed anyway. The flavor really didn't matter at this point.

Maybe she should buy the office the same state-of-the-art

coffeepot she'd purchased for the Chicago Violent Crimes team after they helped her save Michelle.

"Okay, I'm here, so can you tell me now?" Larson fiddled with the rim of his cup but didn't drink. "Is Erick Lucklow dead?"

Lucas sat down with his cup. "I'm sorry to have to tell you that Special Agent Russo and I discovered his body earlier this evening."

Larson flinched as if physically rebuffing the news. While Journey gave him a moment to process, he massaged his forehead as if pushing this new, horrific truth through his skin.

When she judged he'd had enough time, Journey started in. "When was the last time you spoke with Lucklow? You mentioned him vanishing online…recently. Did you stay in touch after the hunting trip?"

Larson's face paled, and his eyes fixed on the table. "Just through Facebook. Pictures of his kid. Vacation photos. That sort of thing."

"What about Faulkner and Perry?" Lucas pulled a face of his own as he sipped the weak coffee. "Did you stay in touch with them?"

"Nah." Larson shrugged, seemingly defeated already by the mere mention of their names. "If they posted anything, I usually saw it." He looked up and opened his mouth as if wanting to say something more, but no sound escaped his lips.

Journey waited patiently, knowing silence could be more persuasive than words.

Ten, fifteen seconds passed until Larson collapsed back in his chair, opened his fists, and flopped his hands palms up on the table. "We weren't all friends. Jerry was my neighbor growing up, and the rest of the guys were *his* hunting buddies. Hell, I don't even know if he was close to them or if they all just had the same hobby."

Lucas knitted his fingers together and leaned forward. "You mean hunting?"

Larson averted his eyes and gazed into the corner. "More like drinking." His voice was a low rumble of regret. "I told those assholes to take it easy."

Journey quietly eased out her notebook and jotted, *alcohol-involved accident*? From what she recalled, there hadn't been any mention of it in the file. "Are you saying you believe alcohol may have played a role in Jerry's accident?"

"I *know* it did." His reaction left no room for misinterpretation.

Journey's mouth had barely opened before Larson jabbed his finger at the folder between her and Lucas. "That report you have there. It's full of lies. That's what cursed us."

She shifted her weight in her chair, eyeing him carefully. "There was no mention of alcohol in the final report. Is that the secret you thought you were taking to your grave?"

"The start of it." Larson dropped his head and ran a hand through his disheveled beard. "Look, everyone else is dead. So I know this is gonna look like me trying to cover my ass. But I've been doing that for years, trying to raise awareness of all the hatin' and cheatin' going on in this world. But sounding the alarm on social media ain't done me no good, and I'd rather spend the rest of my life in jail than look over my shoulder, waiting for whoever murdered them to finally catch me."

Lucas held up his notes, reminding Larson he was on the record. "You are aware of the consequences of anything you're about to say?" Although Larson wasn't under arrest yet, they'd read him his Miranda rights earlier.

"What did I just tell you?" He threw his hands in the air, exasperated. "I'm the only one left! I got nothing to hide."

31

Lucas locked eyes with Larson, sitting across the conference room table. “Okay, Rob. Tell us what happened on that hunting trip. Tell us what’s been haunting you.”

Journey opened her phone and pressed the record button, then stated the date, time, and the names of those present. “Robert Larson, do you agree to have this interview recorded?”

“Yeah, sure.” Larson fumbled with his coffee cup. He shakily brought it to his lips and gulped down its contents in one long swig, as if he needed the caffeine to bolster his courage for telling the story.

“Jerry and I were close as kids. We grew apart, some in high school and college, but never fell out of favor. When I moved back to Pittsburgh after graduating, we picked up where we’d left off. Eventually, he mentions he has this group of guys he goes hunting with and invites me to come along on their weekend trips. So of course, I said yes.”

“How many of these trips did you go on?” Lucas spun his own coffee cup in place on the table with one hand.

“Oh, I don’t know.” Larson shook his head. “But enough

to know the routine. Drive to West Virginia Friday after work. Eat dinner, have a few beers before bed. We were always up before dawn Saturday morning, ready to hunt."

"So only a few beers before bed?" Journey's brow furrowed. "No Friday-night party?"

He twisted the cup in his hands, and his gaze dropped to the chipped table. "The booze they brought only came out after a successful day of hunting."

"They?" Journey repeated the word with emphasis. "Did you not partake?"

"I don't like to mix drinking and firearms. The other guys usually kept it to a celebratory reward for good hunting. Except…that weekend." Larson's head dipped as he hunched in on himself.

Lucas took notes on the conversation, while Journey probed further. "Was there a reason for that weekend's excess?"

"Erick was in the middle of a nasty divorce, and he wasn't coping." Larson sighed. "Before I realize it, he's pouring predawn shots for everyone and packing a bottle of Jack to bring with us to the blinds."

Lucas wrote *shots* and *bottle* in his notes. "Was Erick the only one drinking that morning?"

"More accurate to say I was the only one who wasn't." Larson had an air of mournfulness as he spoke. "Even Sam did a shot. I yelled at him. He owned a freaking gun shop. Hell, he knew better than any of us how reckless that was. What an asshole." His fingers tightened around the empty cup.

Lucas nodded. Faulkner should've known. But if logic and reason were the only things humans relied on when making decisions, Lucas's caseload would have been as light as a feather. "Keep going."

"The morning was surprisingly low-key. I didn't know if

the guys were tired or if the alcohol had mellowed them out, but the hours passed without much notice." Larson began plucking out small bits of Styrofoam from his cup. "I remember there was a buck at the edge of the woods. He must've known we were there because he'd snort, sort of make himself known, and then as soon as we set up a shot, the damn thing would retreat. It was driving the guys nuts. Nobody could get an angle on him."

That was consistent with what Lucas and Journey had already learned from the NPS file.

"By lunch, the guys had finished a bottle of Jack Daniel's. Then Jerry announces he's gotta take a pissah." A smile tugged at Larson's lips as he recounted this memory. "That was Jerry's thing. 'I gotta take a pissah.' Trying to sound like a guy from Boston and dropping the *R*, you know?"

"I know the accent." Journey chuckled. "Pahk the cah in Hahvahd Yahd."

"Yep. Exactly." Larson smiled, but his amusement passed quickly. His scowl returned, and he blew out a slow breath. "Anyway, he climbed down from the blind, and we assumed he went to do his business."

Lucas couldn't stop himself from glancing at Journey, contemplating whether she was going to dig into the question of just how far away was far enough when peeing outdoors.

She remained silent as she hastily scratched something on the paper in front of her, her eyebrows furrowed in concentration.

Larson cleared his throat. "We were busy watching Norman, drunk off his ass, try to take a shot at the buck. Erick said something about seeing a flash of orange. Then Sam shoved him out of the way and told Norman he'd give him the damn rifle if he made the shot."

"What was the flash of orange?" Lucas didn't want to ask, because he already knew.

"I'm getting there." Larson sighed a resigned sigh. "Erick got upset. I don't remember if it was Sam pushing him or the promise of giving Norman a new rifle. He was the reason we were out there…the divorce…separation and all."

"Did Norman take the shot?" Journey inched to the edge of her seat.

"I tried to get the guys to settle down." The strength in Larson's voice vanished. "I wanted Erick to show me where he'd seen that flash of orange. Keep in mind, Jerry had gone down to do his business. None of us knew where he went or how long he'd been gone. I didn't expect he'd be out there, but sometimes there are hikers who get lost and wander into areas they're not supposed to be in."

Larson's eyes began to tear up. He brushed his forearm across his face and took a deep breath before continuing.

"So I yell at the guys to shut up and tried to get a look through my binoculars. I should've been keeping an eye on Norman. It got real quiet while I was trying to find that buck or whatever Erick had seen. And then the rifle went off. Norman took his shot."

"What did he hit?" Lucas met Larson's eyes. The poor man looked haunted.

"At that point, we didn't know." Larson's shoulders slumped. "But I had one of those moments. You know? A bad feeling. And Jerry still hadn't come back."

"That's when you went looking for him? Right after the gun went off?" Journey rested her elbows on the table and leaned her chin into her hands.

"That's not what it says there in the report, I'll bet. See… the guys were teasing Norman. Sam poured him a shot of…I don't remember what liquor he had left. 'His shot of shame.'" Larson air-quoted as he rolled his eyes. "Then Erick took one. And well...Sam couldn't be the only one, besides me, missing out on shots."

"What happened next?" Journey, like Lucas, kept her gaze glued to Larson's face, desperate to hear the rest of the story.

"After a while, we went to go investigate, but it wasn't without a whole lot of yelling." Larson scoffed. "I stashed our guns in the corner and made the guys climb out of the blind. I remember going down the ladder, hopin' and prayin' that Jerry was just pranking us. I'd be mad, but at least I'd know he was okay."

"Was there a strategy for your search?"

"Strategy?" Larson released a frustrated sigh and shook his head. "It was like herding cats. They all went stumbling into the woods, yelling for Jerry at the top of their lungs. And the farther we went, the angrier I got, because I'm not just looking for my friend, you see. I'm babysitting a bunch of drunks." His face flushed, and his jaw muscle throbbed as if he were fighting back emotion.

Lucas fiddled with the clasp on his watch as he tried to imagine how chaotic the scene must've been, with Rob Larson being the only sober one among the group and trying to organize a search party.

"They were tripping on fallen branches and slipping around on patches of mud. It took every ounce of my patience just to keep track of the three of them." Larson ran a shaking hand through his thinning hair and blew out a ragged breath. "With all their hollering, calling Jerry's name and such, there was no chance of us bagging a deer. We scared damn near everything away."

Like that really mattered at that point.

"Then Sam found him." Larson spoke through gritted teeth. "Jerry was lying on his back close to where the buck had been. Norman's shot ripped a giant hole through his middle."

Lucas winced as he let go of the strap on his watch. Gut shots were brutal. "Was he alive when you found him?"

Larson's face contorted in genuine pain. "Not even a little bit."

They remained quiet for a minute. Lucas didn't want to rush Larson's story.

Journey slid a box of tissues across the table toward Larson, who looked as if he were holding back tears.

After a quiet mumble of thanks, Larson took a tissue from the box and wiped his face. "Jerry's head was a mess. His hat had fallen off, and there was blood on his face. Then we saw it. Blood. Bits of brain. Broken skull. It was splattered all over the rock beside him. He must have fallen and hit his head." Larson's breath hitched. He shielded his eyes from view with the tissue. "Jesus. It was awful."

Lucas let him regain his composure before asking what happened next.

"I wanted to call the sheriff or park services. We had to get help immediately. I reached for my cell, but Sam grabbed my wrist and stopped me." Larson balled up the tissue and clenched it. "He had the audacity to remind me they'd all been drinking. As if I'd forgotten. I wanted to punch the guy in the face. He, of all people, knew they shouldn't have been drinking in the first place. And Jerry was dead because of them."

"Was Sam the only one urging you to hold off on calling for help?" Lucas poised his pen, ready for what came next.

"Erick and Norman sort of agreed with me." Larson's lip curled. "Until Sam told them they'd be convicted of manslaughter if the cops discovered they were drinking. I tried to argue that maybe they wouldn't get in trouble. It was an accident. But Sam countered that my opinion didn't matter because I was stone sober and didn't share their risk."

Lucas leaned forward, attempting to keep all judgment from his tone and body language. "So you didn't call it in?"

"How could I?" Larson shrugged in defeat. "If I did, I'd be ruining all their lives. They were fathers with families. I couldn't be the reason they all went to prison."

Lucas nodded in understanding as he scribbled on the page. "So you waited?"

"Yeah." Larson swallowed hard. "The four of us went back to the cabin and waited until everyone sobered up. Then we called nine-one-one and reported that Jerry was dead by the time we found him."

Lucas resisted the temptation to remind Larson that, in the eyes of the law, omitting relevant information was the equivalent of lying. But Rob had been living with the consequences of his lies for the past seven years. The universe had already delivered that lecture.

"I told myself it was better this way because we all had kids, and why make a tragedy even worse by sending those kids' fathers to prison?" He rubbed his forehead again.

Lucas wrote furiously as he watched Larson struggle internally with his conscience.

"I can't imagine what Jerry's son went through. Losing his mom to cancer, then his dad gets shot through the gut by one of his own buddies. That..." He pounded his fist on the table. "That is what's torn me up the most. That kid, Corey."

Lucas perked up. "Did you know him well?"

"When he was a kid. The guys from the neighborhood used to get together for barbecues and such. We'd bring our wives and kids, a package of hot dogs, a six-pack of beer, and spend the day at Riverview Park. Man, it tore me up to watch that boy lose everything. I tried to think about what that would've been like for any of us back in the day. So I used to send him stuff from time to time. Dumb crap, like a picture I found of me and his dad as teenagers or Christmas cards.

That kind of thing. I put my phone number inside and told him if he ever needed anything, just to call me."

Journey's pen, too, was moving in double-time across her page.

Lucas strained to keep his face neutral. "Did he ever?"

"Nah." Larson shook his head. "He's online, though, so I've kept tabs on him. To make sure he's okay. I figure it's the least I can do in Jerry's honor. I was thrilled when he graduated from college. I was starting to worry because for a few years there, every picture Corey posted, well...he was either drinking or getting into some other trouble. Then, boom. He's in his cap and gown and moving to California."

"How long ago was that?"

Larson pinched his lips and sent his gaze toward the ceiling as if in thought. "Maybe a year? He's a programmer for some tech firm. Can't tell you much more than that. Surfing the internet is about as technical as I get."

When Lucas's phone rang, the caller ID showed *San Clemente PD*. He'd been waiting for his old buddy Ramon to call him back about Corey Minton.

Lucas turned to Journey. "Five-minute break?"

32

Melinda Larson blinked in surprise as a loud knock echoed from her front door. It was late on a Saturday night, and she'd already changed into her pajamas and begun her nightly skin-care routine. Cautiously, Melinda stopped her hands mid-lather, her almond-scented face wash dripping down into the sink, and listened closely.

The persistent knocking echoed up the stairs into her bathroom.

It was probably Briella. She rolled her eyes and shook her head.

Saturday nights at the bar were hopping. Briella didn't like working the busier nights. Apparently there were more tips, but they were smaller because she couldn't make a "personal connection." She'd often beg off early.

Normally Briella didn't get home until two in the morning, and she tended to forget her keys. The early-morning pounding on the door to be let in was a habit Melinda had grown increasingly weary of.

This would be the last time she forgave Briella's absentmindedness.

She doused her face with water, patted it dry, threw on a sweatshirt, and padded down the hardwood steps, careful not to slip and crack her head open. She was sock-footed, and at this time of night, she wanted to be sliding under the covers, not running downstairs to open the door for her forgetful roommate.

Melinda stopped at the door, her hand on the cold brass knob, and hesitated a moment. Maybe if she let her roommate stew out there a little longer, she'd get the message and realize what an inconvenience it was to others to constantly forget her keys.

Another series of knocks had Melinda groaning in frustration.

"I swear to god, Briella. This is the last time I'm letting you in."

"Melinda?" A male voice startled her.

She yanked her hand free of the doorknob.

"Are you in there? It's Corey. I hope you remember me. Corey Minton."

Melinda peeked through the peephole and saw him standing under the porch light.

"I know it's late." Corey was shouting through the door now. "I need help and didn't have anywhere else to go."

Maybe it was the tone of his voice, her instincts, or just the time of night. They all told her to pull back. She stepped away from the door.

Is that really him?

Corey had always been a bit of a weird kid when they were growing up. He never really picked up on social cues, and other kids made fun of him for it. But he'd always been nice to her, and Melinda had been raised to treat people with the same respect she would want to receive, so she tolerated him when others couldn't.

Their families had been close, at least until his father

died. He'd been shipped off to live with his grandparents after that, and Melinda lost track of him. It must have been almost a decade since she'd last seen him.

"Sorry, I know it's weird for me to be showing up at your door like this." Sadness ebbed from his voice. Something... his shoulder, head, or some other part of his body...thumped against the door. "I've got nowhere else to go and was having a rough night and just really need a friend, and I knew you were nearby."

She was suddenly aware of the time and not at all eager to entertain guests this late at night. But her dad had always encouraged her to be nice to Corey. Occasionally, she sent Corey a *How ya doing*? pity text. Plus, if she didn't let him in, she was sure her nosy old lady neighbor would call the landlord to complain about the shouting back and forth through the door.

The threat of one more call from management was all the persuading she needed, and against her better instincts, she flipped the lock.

She pasted a veiled smile on her face and opened the door. "C'mon in, Corey."

Looking at her old friend, it surprised her to see how the sixteen-year-old Corey she remembered had aged, looking more haggard than a twenty-three-year-old man should. But he still had the same cowlick that kept that part of his hair perpetually perpendicular.

"Long time no see, I guess."

He made prayer hands as he stepped through. "Thank you so much, Melinda."

She noticed a few angry red patches of skin on his face and hands. Sunburn, maybe? Or an allergic reaction to something? Whatever they were, they looked painful. "It's fine. Just keep your voice down. I don't need the neighbor complaining. She hears everything."

He wiggled an eyebrow. "*Everything?*"

His suggestive tone irked Melinda.

She chided herself almost immediately. It wasn't fair to judge him so quickly. Corey'd had a tough life, and it was no wonder he was a little *off*. Both his parents had died when he was just a kid. He deserved her patience and time to smooth out his rough edges.

Anyway, it wouldn't kill her to help. She knew her dad still occasionally sent him trinkets and kind messages. She could deal with him long enough to get him back to his car and on his way.

"I'm going to run upstairs and grab a blanket so you can crash on the couch." Melinda turned toward the stairs.

Before she could take another step, his hand gripped her ponytail, yanking against her scalp. She gasped as pain shot through her head, her body crashed to the floor, and all the air was knocked out of her lungs.

Corey's sneering face appeared above her. "*Tsk, tsk*. Didn't your self-defense instructor teach you never to wear a ponytail? They're too easy for an attacker to grab."

None of what had just happened made sense.

A wave of dread ran across Melinda as she tried to suck in a breath. She had taken self-defense classes, but this was the first time she'd have to put her skills to use in an actual fight. Her heart beat furiously as she attempted to scramble to her feet.

Corey lunged forward, throwing a punch straight at her face. In a blind panic, she managed to roll away just in time and got to her knees.

"Back off!" Her yell came out shaky. Maybe having a nosy neighbor would finally have an advantage. Every muscle was tense, ready for action as Corey advanced toward her.

He aimed a kick at her head.

Her reflexes kicked in fast, allowing her to duck behind

the couch just in time to hear the force of his foot connect with the furniture instead of her body.

Anger surged through Melinda's veins. With her fists clenched tight, she moved around the couch, coming up behind Corey before he spotted her and sending her foot out. The well-timed roundhouse kick caught Corey in the ribs and sent him sprawling backward.

Disoriented and dazed, he struggled, spitting curses at Melinda as he got back onto his feet.

She'd given it her best shot, but it wasn't enough to take him out.

Corey lunged forward, his fist flying fast and furious. Punch after punch, he pummeled her in the chest, stomach, and ribs. She tried to block them as she backed away, but the living room furniture prevented her escape.

She scrambled, tripping over the coffee table, and went down hard.

Corey was on her. His hands gripped her arms. He held her down, pressing all his weight against her body as he wrapped his arms around her neck in a stranglehold.

His musty breath blew across her face as he leaned closer. "You thought you could fight me? You're nothing more than a weak little girl."

Melinda struggled against Corey's hold, trying to break free. Every breath grew harder to take, and her muscles ached from the strain of such an awkward position. She managed to get one arm out of his grip and tried to push him away from her.

But he was too strong and held her tight.

Her vision blurred as the crushing grip of Corey's bicep pressed against her neck, squeezing her throat closed. Everything slowly faded to black as consciousness slipped away from her.

When Melinda woke up, wooziness and disorientation overwhelmed her. It took a few moments for her surroundings to come into focus. She was in her kitchen, bound with zip ties to the new wrought iron scrollwork bistro chair her roommate Briella had bought for their apartment.

The chair was heavy and solid. There was no getting out, and it almost seemed to mock her for trying. Melinda wished Briella hadn't saved up several weeks' worth of tips to buy the damn bistro set.

Panic set in as Melinda realized what had happened, but before she could scream for help, Corey appeared in front of her with a gun and a satisfied smirk.

She stared at the weapon in horror, unable to move or speak.

Corey looked at Melinda for several long seconds. "This is how we're gonna play it." He began freeing one of her hands. "You're going to call your old man. Get him to come down here. Don't tell him why. Understood?" He shoved her phone in her face.

Melinda let out a squeak as she nodded.

He pressed the gun to her forehead. "I swear...if you try anything funny, I'll put a bullet in your head."

She froze in place, fearing that any sudden movement, even a nod, would be enough to set him off.

"Make the call."

The phone nearly fell from her trembling fingers as she started to dial her father's number.

33

Lucas paced the hallway, phone pressed to his ear as he listened to his old navy buddy turned police detective.

"Officers stopped by Corey Minton's apartment, but they didn't locate him. A neighbor said he hasn't been around in weeks. I confirmed that with his landlord. Corey was up to date on his rent, but his mailbox had filled to the point that the post office put a hold on further deliveries."

Lucas grunted in response. "And what about his car?"

"A Toyota Tacoma, registered to Corey Minton." Ramon paused, and Lucas made out the sound of keys clacking. "Records show it was towed off the street for parking violations and has been sitting in impound since March twenty-sixth."

"Thanks for all your help on this one, Ramon. I owe you one." Lucas disconnected the call and dashed over to his and Journey's shared desk space, immediately searching for Minton's name in the FAA database.

If his vehicle was impounded in California, he'd have most likely flown to Pennsylvania. Assuming he's here.

"Come out, come out, wherever you are, Corey Minton.

We have some questions for you." Lucas couldn't find any airplane tickets in Corey's name. Driving to Pittsburgh from the West Coast was a multi-day trip, complicated exponentially by the fact that the only car he'd found registered in Corey's name had been sitting in an impound lot for three weeks.

Maybe he was wrong to suspect Corey was in Pennsylvania.

Then again, there were plenty of ways to get yourself across the country if you wanted it bad enough.

Realizing the five minutes he'd requested had passed, Lucas returned to the conference room with his laptop, a couple of sodas, and a bag of trail mix. "Sorry, that took longer than I expected, but I grabbed some snacks."

Journey stood just as Lucas sat down and headed for the door. "My turn. Be back in a minute. Need anything else from the vending machine?"

"More snacks are always welcome." Lucas slid the bag of trail mix and a can of soda across the table.

"Thanks." Larson cracked open the drink and sipped the fizz from the top. "So what's going to happen to me now that our lies have been exposed? Do I take the fall for everyone?" The question came out flat without a hint of bitterness. No self-pity in his tone.

He looked like a decent man who'd fought the good fight and lost. Wrinkles too deep for his forty-seven years, clothes threadbare at the edges. He'd left the wrinkled and stained flannel at home, but the t-shirt beneath confirmed the story the top layer had told, that life had been difficult and showed no signs of easing.

"The record will have to be corrected, and the D.A. will decide whether to bring any charges. It's not up to Agent Russo or me, but I'll do what I can to advocate on your behalf."

The defeat, Larson's complete resignation to his fate, struck Lucas harder than he expected, a direct shot to the heart. He'd learned to accept that his job would always have fewer black-and-white answers than shades of gray.

Would time behind bars teach this guy more of a lesson than he's already learned?

That wasn't up to Lucas to judge.

"You don't need to do that. I took part in the lie. And I think we'd both agree that going to prison is better than what happened to Sam, Norman, and Erick. Maybe I deserve the same." Larson ran a hand down his face.

Lucas empathized with the guy. Larson had been so broken down by life, he wondered if he deserved to die. "That's a pretty tough way to look at it."

"Probably." Larson tore open the trail mix and poured a few pieces into his hand, shaking them like dice. "Then again, the secrets ruined my marriage, my job. The mental stress of rationalizing what we did took a toll every day. It's awful enough to see one of your oldest friends lying dead on the ground, shot in the gut, blood everywhere. But then to play an active role in the cover-up...it's a road to insanity."

The nuts and candy bobbed in his palm, a mesmerizing swirl of color.

"My wife, Pauline, and I made a promise before we got married. No secrets between us, no matter how hard it gets. We kept that promise for sixteen years. Until I broke it. I did it for her sake, obviously. To keep her from being a party to our crime. But every day of our marriage after that became a lie because I knew I wasn't living up to the ethical and moral standards I'd set for myself as a man. As a father, I'd have to discipline my daughter for lying about small, rather inconsequential matters, all the while hiding my dishonesty."

"Sounds rough." It wasn't Lucas's job to bond with the guy, but he couldn't help but witness his pain.

"If there's anything I'd tell my daughter now, it's that a lie, even a small one, trickles into everything. Every little part of your life. It's why I lost my mojo in sales. I was an incredible salesman, busted through my quotas every month. Then I realized that in order to sell, I had to believe in my product, which is hard to do when you can't believe in yourself anymore."

Lucas nodded. "What did you sell?"

Larson chuckled. "Everything at one point or another. Sold cars to pay my way through college. Office supplies. Insurance packages. Large equipment. But I made my money in medical equipment. We bought our house on the commissions from a tiny switch cardiologists used to regulate a patient's artificial heart valve."

"A whole house from a tiny switch. That's impressive." Lucas hadn't gone into law enforcement for the money, but sometimes the discrepancy between public service and private enterprise reared up before his eyes.

"Yeah. Except the minute a salesman questions his pitch, it's over. I'd known there were risks with this valve since I started selling it. Everything comes with risks, and I was always careful to disclose them. Like I said, I envisioned myself as an ethical man. Then, after Jerry died and the guilt kicked in, I couldn't get the risks out of my head. Once, near the end, I had a huge cardiology practice down in San Antonio on the hook for a major sale, like a couple million dollars, and I actually asked them if they were really sure they wanted to buy."

Lucas's jaw dropped. "So much for your next house."

"So much for my job." Larson smiled so wide his eyelids shrank to slits. "My boss fired me before I got on the plane to fly home. And rightly so." He finally popped the trail mix from his hand into his mouth. Just as his phone lit up. "Um."

He held the screen up for Lucas to see. "It's my daughter. Do you mind if I take it? It's unusual for her to call this late."

If Hallie called him past nine, Lucas broke out in a sweat, so he completely understood what Larson meant. "Go ahead."

Larson was grinning as he answered. "Hey, love. What's up?"

Lucas opened his laptop and busied himself with forms, of which there was never any shortage.

Journey returned, holding a package of candy in one hand and a protein bar in the other. "Take your pick." She held them out for Lucas to choose.

"Halfsies?" Lucas arched an eyebrow.

"I like your style, Special Agent Sullivan." Journey smiled mischievously. As they split their snacks, she nodded toward Larson. "Who's on the phone?"

"His daughter. Given how late it is, I let him take it."

"Whoa, whoa." Larson jumped to his feet. "Slow down. Tell me what's happening."

Lucas's heart leaped into his chest at the sound of fear in Larson's voice. His instincts as both a father and an investigator piqued.

"Hold on. What…say again?" Larson's voice sharpened with urgency, and his gaze darted from side to side, searching for answers. "You're slurring."

Journey wrote *drinking* on Lucas's notepad and lifted her eyebrows in question.

He shrugged.

Lucas's mind shifted into overdrive as he fought to understand Larson's chaotically panicked monologue.

"Baby girl, calm down. I'm trying to understand." Larson began to pace back and forth across the room. "How can I help if I don't know…?" He stopped dead in his tracks. "Okay.

I'll be there. I promise." His face drained of all color as he hung up the phone.

Lucas and Journey exchanged worried glances.

"Something's wrong." Larson clutched his chest as he sucked in deep, heaving breaths. "She's upset and needs me to go to her apartment."

Journey got up and stepped in front of the door. "We can't let you go right now."

"I'm not trying to run." Larson approached the chair across from them and loomed there, wringing his hands with anxious anticipation. "I'll pay for my crimes if necessary, but my baby girl's in trouble. I have to help her."

"What kind of trouble? Was she drinking? Did she get into an accident?" Lucas stood as well. "You said she sounded like she was slurring."

"No." Larson shook his head emphatically. "Not like drunk slurring. More like panic screeching. I'm not sure what's happened, but she needs help."

"Let's take a breath." Journey mimed the motion for Larson. "Go over the conversation with us. What exactly did she tell you?"

"We've always had a code word, you know." Larson pressed the heels of his hands against his temples, as if to keep his head from exploding. "Since Melinda was little. If she told us she was 'phlegmy,'" he air-quoted, "it meant she was in trouble and needed help."

Lucas completely understood that. Back when Hallie was little, Serena had suggested they come up with a word like that too. Something that could be said in everyday conversation without alerting suspicion, but for Serena, Hallie, and him, it meant "Help me."

"So she's in trouble." Journey crossed her arms. "But did she say what kind?"

"I think so, but I don't know." Larson scratched his head.

"It's complicated. Silly code words and whatnot. But she said she was phlegmy. That means she needs my help."

"What else did she say with it?" Lucas asked. "Maybe there was a clue in the rest of her words to tell you what kind of trouble."

"Uh...I'm not sure." Larson fidgeted uncomfortably beneath Lucas's and Journey's scrutinizing gazes, as though his thoughts had gotten stuck inside his head, and he couldn't figure out how to get them out.

Lucas half expected to see steam rising from Larson's ears as hard as he appeared to be thinking.

Then finally, Larson exhaled a defeated breath. "She said she burned her throat on berry cobbler."

"Does any of that have any significant meaning to you?" Lucas leaned in. "Was berry cobbler something she hated?"

"Just the opposite. Back when Melinda was little, she used to gobble that stuff up faster than candy. Caroline Minton used to bake some of the best cobbler. One year Melinda asked..." Larson's eyes widened. "She asked Caroline to bake a cobbler for her birthday instead of a cake."

"Caroline Minton. As in Corey Minton's mother?" Journey looked at Lucas, as if they were thinking the same thing.

Lucas wasn't much of a gambling man, but he'd put money on that cobbler being Melinda's way of saying Corey Minton was the reason for her frantic call.

34

Melinda stared up at Corey, who walked around the kitchen in agitated circles while muttering to himself. He'd been such a quiet boy. A little shy and awkward, but never in a million years could she have imagined he would turn out to be the devil.

Now he circled her with an evil glint in his eye and a gun clenched tightly in his fist.

He'd made her summon her father to his death.

How had he changed from such a trusting soul into this menacing figure? It was all Melinda could do not to crumble as guilt coursed through her veins. By doing Corey's bidding, she'd condemned her father to doom. And even though she'd done it under a threat of violence, part of her knew that if her father died, some of the responsibility would rest on her shoulders.

"Just kill me now." She spat the words at him. "Why wait for my father to get here?"

Corey had the nerve to smile as he took her phone and slipped it into his pocket. "I can't kill you. We're not finished yet."

Melinda was certain she'd scared her father. There was a chance, only a small one, that he'd recognized the code she'd used. Maybe he was calling the police. She hadn't used their family code word in so long, and he might not have remembered it.

Even as that thought crossed her mind, she knew it was a lie. The conviction in her father's voice when she'd told him she was phlegmy was unmistakable. He knew what that meant.

But did he recognize what she was hinting at when she said she'd burned her mouth on the berry cobbler? That wasn't anything they'd set up, but Melinda couldn't just come out and say Corey was holding her at gunpoint. The best she could do was hint at Corey's mother's delicious berry cobbler.

It hurt Melinda's heart to think of that sweet woman. Taken too early by cancer.

Would Corey have turned out to be a killer if his mother had lived? Losing both of his parents had clearly influenced him. Turned him into a monster.

For a split second, Melinda flashed on the idea of acting the role of the consoling woman from all the crime dramas she'd watched. Maybe she could de-escalate the situation by giving Corey a person to talk to. Someone to listen to all the hardship he'd endured. Show a little sympathy for how he'd tragically lost his family.

Maybe with the right words, she could win his trust.

But try as she might, Melinda couldn't drum up a single bit of empathy for the man threatening her with a gun.

A gun he would surely turn on her father the moment he stepped through the front door.

Maybe he wouldn't come.

Her mind kept circling to that hopeful thought, but she knew the truth.

He'd called her "baby girl." Like a secret code between them, it was his way of saying he would do anything to help her. The recognition made Melinda want to curl into herself and disappear.

Her memory flashed to an afternoon when she was a child. The three of them, her mom included, had been running errands, and Melinda was acting rambunctious and couldn't sit still in the shopping cart.

Her dad gave her a peck on the cheek and offered to take her to the playground so her mom could finish shopping.

Melinda remembered her father's big hand around hers, the safety in it. The neighborhood mall had a children's area filled with plastic woodland creatures shaped into slides, swings, and rocking horses. On an average Saturday, it overflowed with dads and their kids. She and her father inevitably ended up there every weekend too. Which was probably, she realized now, the entire reason she'd been acting up that day in the first place.

Her favorite part of the play area was the spinning turtle, a child-propelled merry-go-round. One kid would grab a handle and push, running round and round, while the others stood atop the spinning shell, hanging on for dear life.

Melinda always preferred to ride rather than run, the pint-size daredevil she was.

That day the kid pushing the ride was stronger than usual, and they reached a speed she couldn't handle. Her small fingers were no match for the increasing centrifugal force. Melinda remembered flying off, cackling with laughter as she went airborne. It wasn't until she hit the ground and her knee erupted in blood that her giggles turned to tears. She wailed for her dad to save her, and he did.

He was at her side in an instant, eyes glistening with care and devotion as he doctored her. That was the first time he'd called her his "baby girl." He promised he would always be there to pick her up when she fell down. That memory stuck with her. From that moment on, Melinda knew without a doubt that her father would be there to help, no matter what.

Corey impatiently checked his watch. "How far away does Daddy live?"

"Thirty minutes." It was more like ten. *Maybe Dad can catch him by surprise.*

"Don't tell me he let his little darling move a whole thirty minutes away. That's not a very good father, if you ask me." The look in Corey's eyes was pure evil. "Then again, what would I know about having a father?" He reached behind her to check the ties around her ankles.

She had to do something. This might be her only chance.

Melinda threw herself at him, driving her head straight into his face.

"You fucking bitch." Corey scrambled back, a trickle of blood racing down from his reddened nose. His eyes flashed with a look of pure hatred as he pointed the gun at her.

She barely heard the report, and even after the sound had reached her ears, Melinda wasn't fully aware of what had happened, but a sharp pain ran through her abdomen. Blood bubbled out of the wound in her belly, and a slow, searing fire licked its way up her chest.

She'd been shot.

Melinda was still upright. The ties at her wrists and feet kept her from sliding out of the chair as shock took over. Warm blood spread across her body, and a strange sense of detachment washed over her.

Corey pulled out the second kitchen chair and placed it in front of her. Then he sat down and watched her helplessly bleed onto the floor. He grinned. "When you asked me to kill you, I didn't expect you'd end up doing most of the work."

35

Journey and Lucas sped down the Pittsburgh streets for the second time that night. Homes and businesses were little more than a blur as they headed for Melinda Larson's residence.

Larson had pleaded to come along. He'd even promised to stay in the car while they handled the scene. A distraught father, however, was the last ingredient Journey wanted to add to an already murky, and possibly murderous, stew.

Journey coordinated with SSA Kenner, who would be following with the tactical team.

Lucas pulled onto the highway and accelerated beyond the posted speed limit. "What do we know?"

"Melinda Larson was slurring when she called her father." Journey read from the notes on her phone as Larson texted over some quick facts about Melinda's town house. "That suggests she might be injured or under the influence of something. She also alluded to Corey Minton being in the apartment with her message of needing help."

"Anyone else in the house we should be aware of?" Lucas weaved through traffic. "Roommates or boyfriends?"

"She has a roommate, so we may encounter a woman named Briella. She's got blue hair and is about a foot taller than Melinda, according to Larson." As soon as Journey swiped past one message from Larson, another popped up. "But he needs to stop texting in single lines. I know he's a frantic father, but it's so hard for me to keep up."

Her phone vibrated again, and Journey let out a frustrated growl.

"Tactical and SWAT are on the way." She read off the message she'd just received from Kenner. "They're about seven minutes behind us, though. Kenner says we have point. SWAT will go on our say, if necessary, but we're to evaluate and negotiate first, since we don't have confirmation of a hostage situation."

Lucas pressed down hard on the accelerator. "We're assuming it's Corey Minton inside, and he's expecting Rob to knock on the door."

The GPS momentarily interrupted the conversation with an alert that they were three minutes away.

"We shouldn't make assumptions just yet. But, yes, whoever's inside...they're expecting Rob Larson to come knocking."

"I'd put money on him being our guy. Three out of four men who were with Jerry Minton on that hunting trip have been murdered. The park ranger who took statements on the day Jerry Minton was killed has also been murdered. It sounds to me like young Corey is working his way through the people involved in his father's death."

"But Melinda wasn't on the hunting trip. Why's she being targeted, then?" Journey's mind churned with ideas as she countered. "You think he's trying to flush her father out?"

Lucas kept his eyes on the road as he nodded. "If Corey's in Pennsylvania, and if he's responsible for murdering Hudson, Faulkner, Perry, and Lucklow, then it's a logical conclusion he's drawing Larson out. He wants them all dead."

"Those are some big *ifs*." But Journey couldn't deny that Lucas's theory proved sound. "Play it out for me. Why would Corey be behind this?"

Lucas exited the freeway. "The way I see it, we've got a guy who's fourteen when his mom dies of cancer. That's a tender age for any child, and it's a genuine tragedy. But we know Corey and his dad make a life together on their own... one year without her, then two. Corey might have just learned to live without his mother and recognized that maybe growing up in an all-male house isn't so bad. And then, *bam*!"

He smacked the steering wheel so hard Journey jumped.

"Suddenly, his dad is gone, killed in a grisly hunting accident. Corey is all alone. No mom. No dad. Only now, he's sixteen, the age when a boy's testosterone is fully loaded and ready to take on the world, screwing with his body and his mind and telling him to act like a man just as his role model for what it means to be a man is stolen from him."

The psychology of loss suddenly became very personal, a little too close to home for Journey. She'd been thirteen when she lost her family. But any age was tender when it came to a tragedy like that. "Keep going."

"We know his grandparents raised him, so he wasn't subjected to the foster care system and all the chaos that can bring. But we have observations from Larson that Corey partied a lot throughout his teens. So much so that Rob worried about the kid's future."

Journey had gone through her rebellious phase, and she had to swallow back her ever-present shame about having run off to meet a boy, only to return later that night to find her house a smoldering ruin and her parents and sister dead.

Their cat was the only part of her family she'd saved that evening.

Lucas continued. "What we don't know is whether he pulled himself together. He graduated, and Larson said it appears he has a decent job out in California. In the tech industry. He's a techie."

"Ah, yes, California." Journey chuckled as she rubbed her palms against her slacks, trying to overshadow her shame with a physical sensation. "The land of sunshine, new beginnings, and serial killers."

Lucas eyed her. "He fits the profile."

Journey nodded. "If it *is* Corey inside, he'll most likely be armed with any number of the guns stolen from Sam Faulkner's place."

The GPS directed them to turn onto Melinda's street just as Journey got a text from the tactical team that they were now five minutes away. She got another text, and her stomach clenched.

"Shit. Nine-one-one got a report of shots fired at Melinda's address."

"Dammit." Lucas parked a few hundred yards down the block to maintain stealth. "Doesn't mean she's dead, though."

Journey had already thought of that. "I can't see him killing his bait. Do you?"

Lucas shook his head. "Nope."

Donning her FBI jacket, vest, and earpiece, Journey set her phone to silent. She looked at Lucas while putting on her gloves. "We've got five minutes. Tactical is listening on channel two."

Lucas double-checked his equipment before confirming the open channel for communication between them and the tactical team.

Journey checked her radio and switched to the open channel. "Let's complete a perimeter sweep of the area."

Melinda's town house was in a tasteful mid-century neighborhood consisting of rows of redbrick duplexes covered in ivy that converged around a central square. Walkways ran between the units and across an expansive communal lawn pocked with barbecue pits and picnic tables.

Armed with Larson's detailed description, they approached silently on foot. The duplex apartment was one half of a town house, with a living room, dining room, and kitchen on the main floor and two bedrooms and a bath upstairs. The front door opened directly into the home, but there was also a screened porch around the side. It opened onto a small rear entryway behind the kitchen.

The porch had been Larson's only security concern when Melinda moved in. He'd told them about the flimsy lock on the screen door and the twist lock on the main door into the house. If someone broke in, chances were, they went in that way.

Journey and Lucas hunched behind a row of bushes in the neighboring yard and watched for signs of movement within the house.

Both floors of the apartment were lit, and that fact alone gave Journey a jolt of optimism. "She's got nearly every bulb in the place burning." There were lights on in every room except one, meaning they wouldn't be clearing dark spaces. It increased their security immensely.

Lucas inched closer. "And there's movement behind the windows."

She'd clocked it too. Judging by Larson's description, someone had just walked across the dining room. "If they cross in front of the windows on the right, they're in the living room. If not, they may have gone upstairs."

As if hearing what she'd said, a light clicked on in a second-floor window.

"That's the bathroom window. Remember, Melinda has a roommate."

"Noted." Lucas's voice was firm yet level. "We have to be prepared for a third person inside."

"I'm going to head around the side and see if I can't get a better view in." Journey adjusted the buckles on her vest. "Larson said there were larger windows and a possible easy entrance at the back of the house."

"Make it quick. Tactical is almost here."

36

Journey understood why a twentysomething would want to live in these town house apartments. Spring and summer weekends probably sprouted as many parties as they did fresh grass and flowers in the central square courtyard. But that same open space put her at risk of getting spotted. There was nothing better to complicate a situation than a self-appointed neighborhood watch on the lookout for a prowler.

Hopefully, none of Melinda's neighbors were playing guard dog tonight.

She sprinted across the square and dove for a hydrangea bush beneath the kitchen window on the side of the house. She rested with her back against the cool brick wall for a few seconds and caught her breath. Her butt sank into the nearly sopping wet soil, which wasn't covered by a thick layer of mulch like she'd expected.

There were no calls, no sudden lights or sounds of windows opening so someone could get a better look at where she was hidden.

Careful to keep her phone screen covered so no one would spot the glow, she checked the time.

Four and a half minutes left.

Plenty of time. If she didn't sit around in the mud smelling the flowers.

Overhead, light shined through the window and cast twisted shadows from the horizontal blinds onto the grass. She listened, but only the electric buzz of the streetlights met her ears.

Getting a look into the room would be tricky, especially with the bush being right beneath it. If she put her face directly in front of the glass, she risked those inside spotting her, and she couldn't back up more than a few inches without landing in the halo of lamplight. Bumping into the giant flowering shrub would cause the branches to sway, giving her away even if she wasn't seen directly.

Her only choice was to move to the far corner of the window and peer in sideways. The angle limited her view to half of the room at a time, and she had to check from both angles, easing around the plant to reach the other side for a full idea of what she was seeing.

What she glimpsed was destruction.

The white cupboards on the left side of the window hung open. Broken dishes lay scattered beneath them on the counter. Across the room, the midsize kitchen table sat empty. Two chairs were tucked in neatly. A third was in the corner, facing the wall. At the sink, the faucet had been left running, as if someone had been washing those broken dishes but then got distracted.

What she didn't see was Melinda.

Journey maneuvered her gaze through the bushes, stopping short when she heard a thump from inside the wreck of a kitchen. A man's voice followed that sudden noise.

"You're going to have to buy a new towel. I'll be taking this one with me."

Journey couldn't view the guy from her current angle and had to move around the bush to get to the other side of the window. That angle had her looking toward the wall that separated the kitchen from the front room.

Inside, a young man paced the gap between rooms, blotting his face with a towel.

Journey kept her voice to a whisper as she keyed her radio. "I have eyes on our perp. Description matches what we have for Corey Minton. He is armed. I can see the gun tucked into the waistband of his jeans."

Corey Minton might have been in his early twenties, but he had the face of a much older man. His skin was more gray than pink or beige, as if he hadn't eaten well in months. His eyes, the skin around them red as if burned, were those of a person who'd seen too much for his years, his mouth seemingly locked in a snarl.

Lucas's voice came through the earpiece. "Do you have eyes on Melinda Larson? Can you confirm the location of Corey Minton in the apartment?"

She'd just opened her mouth when she heard someone respond to Corey's towel rant. This second voice was much quieter and softer, also at a higher pitch.

Journey guessed it was female. Based on what she could make out, the woman speaking had to be near the exterior kitchen door. Tucked into the small corner of the room. Journey couldn't quite get her eyes on her.

At least four feet of the room were obstructed from her vantage point.

Journey strained to make out what the woman was saying. No identifiable words came through, but she picked up on hints of pleading desperation in her weak mumbles.

"No visual yet on Melinda Larson." Journey pressed her head harder against the wall, trying in vain to view that back corner. "I can hear a woman in distress who seems to be talking with our perp. Possibly in the kitchen, but I can't confirm. I'm going to try farther back to see if there's a better view. Hold tactical until my signal."

"Confirmed." There was no hint of hesitation in Lucas's voice. They might be new to working with each other, but they both knew how to follow SOP and properly get their jobs done.

One thing was clear. The woman inside was in trouble. Her voice came across as so pitiful. Journey didn't bother to waste what little time she had left by checking the clock. She already sensed they were running out of time.

What had Corey done to her?

Journey approached the screen door of the back patio area. Reaching forward blindly, she found the knob, a flimsy aluminum handle with a slider lock. She placed her palm against the metal to mute the noise as best she could and gave it a quick yank.

The latch failed to hold, just as Larson had predicted, and the door popped open right into her hand. Unfortunately, the back door to the apartment appeared to be solid oak. Journey crouched low and crept up next to it, pressing her ear to its surface.

Corey was still talking, but his words were muffled through the wood. If the woman was responding, Journey could no longer hear her. Corey came across as manic, barely stopping for breath, so she couldn't blame his hostage for falling silent. Journey used his distraction to her advantage.

Turning on her pocket light, she tucked the end in her mouth before she pulled out her lock-picking kit and assessed the mechanical challenge before her. The dead bolt was so new, it was still shiny and had zero scratches on its face. Larson had been right about a lot of things, but not this. Melinda had taken her father's advice to replace it after all.

Good girl.

If only it had kept her safer tonight.

She slid the hook pick into the lock and ran it gently down the tumbler, getting a feel for the pins. They moved smoothly, giving up their secrets without a fight. Less than ten seconds later, there was a *click*, and the hook pick shifted. *Open sesame.* Journey turned the hook, sliding the dead bolt out of the lock plate without a sound.

She took a breath and gently pushed against the door. Even as her mind shouted at her to stop, to wait for backup, she kept pushing.

Wood scraped on wood with a soft screech that sounded loud enough to wake the dead.

Journey reached for the gold ace of diamonds pendant hanging from her neck and rubbed it for luck as she held her breath and listened for any sound from inside.

Corey's frantic chatter ceased.

Journey willed him to ignore his instincts and go back to his mad ranting.

After what felt like an eternity of silence, he resumed talking.

She exhaled the breath she'd been holding.

Wait. Tactical will be here any minute.

Pulling up on the handle and shifting the angle of its hinges, Journey pushed the door anyway. She just couldn't sit here doing nothing. A minute in this type of situation could cost an innocent young woman her life.

The door moved with less friction and reduced the screech to a dull, muted scuff. This time she used her whole body pressed against the door to muffle the sound as she slowly pushed it open.

Stepping lightly, she maneuvered into the small mudroom space between the patio and the kitchen.

Journey crouched low in the corner and peeked around the wall into the kitchen. Any movement she made beyond her tiny corner would be easy to spot, but she had a clear view of the perp as he paced the kitchen.

Inside the house, she was too close to use the radio without risking Corey hearing her, but she needed to get this information to the tactical team. Waiting 'til he turned and paced the other way, Journey pulled her phone out of her pocket, once again keeping the light hidden, and fired off a message to Lucas. They should arrive any moment now, and he could pass on the information to them instead.

Eyes on perp, gun holstered, pacing the kitchen. Female victim injured and bound in kitchen back corner near the rear entrance. Direct line of sight from front door to center of kitchen. Breach on my signal. Make it loud to distract. I have backdoor access. Will attempt extraction. Confirm message when read.

Turning her phone to video mode, she propped it on the wall with the camera lens barely peeking around the corner. This way, she could not only record the action but also watch Corey without risking him seeing a human face.

"If I'd been thinking more clearly, I wouldn't even be here." Corey spun back to continue his pacing, moving in and out of Journey's line of sight. "Coming here to her apartment was a bad idea."

She couldn't tell who he was speaking to. So far, she hadn't seen any earbuds in his ears or a phone in his hands, so he couldn't be chatting with someone that way.

But the way he spoke flowed too much like a conversation. Maybe he was simply talking to himself. Except he seemed to be losing whatever argument he was having.

"What if that old lady next door called the cops? And Melinda has a roommate. What if she comes home too?"

He seemed to be listening to someone else inside before throwing up his hands.

"I know. With the others, I was in and out after a few

minutes. But here, I'm a sitting duck, waiting for trouble. Coming for Melinda made everything worse. Why did I do this? She isn't who I'm after anyway. Melinda did nothing wrong. Right?"

Journey tried to make sense of what she'd just heard. At this point, she had to assume the woman bound to the chair in the corner of the room was Melinda. If that was the case, why was Corey talking about her in the third person?

He's insane. That's why.

"You're right. Of course I figured Larson was on to me." Corey dropped his head as if he were giving up. "Larson might not have pieced everything together, but he definitely would have reported me to the police after I killed Erick."

It was always nice to hear your suspect admit that your theory about them was right.

Even better when that confession was being recorded and could be used against them in a court of law.

"Can you just stop criticizing me for a moment, please? Let me think!" His tone turned angry, setting off Journey's internal alarms.

The pauses that happened between his angry outbursts were really getting to her. He was talking as if to someone in the room with him, and he had to let them finish speaking before he could respond. Was he talking to voices only he could hear?

Journey's phone flashed a silent alert.

Message received. SWAT moving into position. Breech on your mark.

Carefully holding the phone against the wall, she fired off a one-handed reply.

Be advised. Perp agitated. Delusional. Arguing with shadows. Possible drug influence.

"Maybe instead of killing Rob, I should just kill his daughter." Corey's voice filled with excitement at that prospect. "Keep him alive but make him endure the same torture as me. Knowing how she died. Having to picture it, like a snuff film. Shit, why didn't I think of that earlier? You're a genius!"

The woman in the corner moaned and slumped lower against the restraints holding her in the chair.

She's not going to last much longer.

"Why?" His voice rose to a shout. "Because look at her. She's going to be dead by the time her father gets here."

Her father? He's definitely talking about Melinda.

Those words confirmed the identity of the woman bound to the chair. And with the implied threat he'd just made, there was no more time to waste.

Breech now!

A second after Journey fired off the last text message, there was a crash at the front of the house, followed by loud yelling. "FBI! On the ground, now!"

Journey bolted from her hiding spot and sprang into the kitchen. "FBI! Drop your weapon and get on the ground." She moved to put herself as a physical barrier between the perpetrator and the bound woman in the corner of the kitchen as she raised her service weapon.

With SWAT pouring in through the front door and the rest of the tactical team coming around the side of the house, Corey was surrounded.

Wild eyed and cornered, he spun in circles and pulled the gun from his waistband. "Back up! Everyone just back the hell up." He pointed the gun at Journey's face.

Journey's call was made a split-second later, and she fired off a shot.

The bullet grazed up his gun arm, and he dropped the weapon. But he howled in pain and launched himself at her. She fired a second time. From his grunt, she'd hit again, but she couldn't tell where.

His new wound didn't stop him though.

With his arms locked around her shoulders, he tackled Journey to the ground. Her gun fell from her hand as she hit the wooden floor. Adrenaline pumped through her veins, feeding the strength she needed to scramble.

Journey planted her left foot and pistoned her hips up against Corey's body, giving her enough leverage to rotate and roll on top of him. She sprawled as heavy as she could, using her splayed weight to keep Corey pinned face down under her.

With her on top, the unforgiving floor below, and blood leaking out from the gunshot wound in his leg, it was harder for Corey to move. Blood smeared everywhere, making him and the floor slippery. She used that factor to her advantage, sliding her arm over his to keep it pinned down.

His body twisted beneath her, ragged breaths coming in grunts from between his gritted teeth as he thrashed and flailed like a man possessed.

She strained to control his arm and keep the gun pointed at the baseboard as the rest of the SWAT team shouted in reaction, shuffling for position around them.

Corey stretched out his uninjured hand for her dropped gun.

Time slowed to a crawl as she caught sight of Lucas closing in.

The perp lifted his hand, finger on the trigger.

Journey's heart pounded. If Corey managed to get a shot off, he might hit Lucas. She couldn't let that happen. "Drop your weapon!"

Corey ignored her. With a powerful heave, Corey cried out as he threw all his body weight to the side. His elbow rammed into Journey's chest, winding her as it knocked her back.

While she gasped for breath, Corey scrambled to get to

his hands and knees, slapping the bloody ground as he tried to rise. But before he could fully reach his weapon, Lucas's heavy boot slammed down on his hand like thunder, and the gun skimmed across the floor.

"Mother!" Corey howled as he clutched his injured hand. "Help me, Mother." The young man continued calling for his mom like a frightened child until the wail of ambulance sirens drowned out his cries.

37

Melinda couldn't open her eyes. She begged her brain and ordered her eyelids to obey.

There was nothing but darkness.

Had all the horrors she'd endured robbed her of her sight?

That thought alone was enough to send chills down her spine. She attempted to move but couldn't even lift a finger. Her muscles wouldn't listen, leaving her trapped in her own skin.

This isn't happening.

She strained and tried to thrash her head against the pillow. But only her soft whimpers filled the silent space.

"Melinda. Baby girl. We're here." Her father's voice reached through the darkness like a lifeline. "You're okay. You're safe."

What was happening to her?

She tried to speak, but all Melinda managed were hoarse whispers that barely escaped her lips.

"Relax, baby girl." Her father cooed. "You've been through a lot."

Her mother's voice followed. "You need your rest."

She was safe. Even in the darkness. Their voices were proof of that.

And yet, as she drifted away, fear and confusion lingered in every fiber of her being.

Is it really over?

Melinda woke to the stark glare of a fluorescent light. As her eyes adjusted, they locked onto the familiar face of her father. He smiled softly and followed that up with a gentle embrace. His warm hug was there to ease away any worries.

"We have visitors." Her mother's voice cut through the room, causing Melinda to twist her head, sending a shock through her aching skull. She attempted to rise, but her exhausted body collapsed beneath her.

Every muscle screamed in agony, as if it'd been eons since she'd last moved them. She recognized the tight grasp of medication numbing her senses, but when she stirred, so did the pain.

Still, she managed a smile as her dad welcomed the two guests with open arms.

"Honey," her mother leaned closer in a chair at her side, "these are the FBI agents who saved you."

"Did they get him?" The words scratched raw in Melinda's throat.

"Yes." Her mom squeezed her hand. "You're safe."

After a few more moments of hugs and tear-filled thanks from her parents, the agents moved to Melinda's bedside to introduce themselves.

"I'm Special Agent Journey Russo."

The woman was too tall for Melinda to take her in without straining her eyes. She grimaced as she tried.

Special Agent Russo backed up a few steps. "This better? You've been through a lot."

"Thanks."

"I'm Special Agent Lucas Sullivan." His voice was warm, yet there was a hint of caution. "We were the agents at your apartment last night. You're a very smart and brave young woman."

Doesn't feel that way. Shame overwhelmed Melinda as she looked at the tubes snaking out of her body. Her mind spun, displaying memories she'd rather forget.

"We were hoping to have a chat with you about what happened. Get your statement." Agent Sullivan held a notebook open to a page scribbled with one- and two-word sentences. A single name at the top. *Corey Minton.*

Fear ran through Melinda's veins, mixed with a strange kind of excitement.

Agents Russo and Sullivan told her Corey was in custody, accused of murdering four men as well as charged for felony theft and the illegal sale of firearms. As soon as they had more information on her assault, they'd add that to the litany of charges.

Melinda closed her eyes, tears burning on the surface. She was filled with hatred, something she never thought she would experience. She wanted justice for herself and his other victims. Yet, even as she wished for retribution, pain twisted within her soul.

Hate wasn't a natural feeling for her. It was strange...but also exactly right. Yes. She did hate him. And he needed to pay for what he'd done.

Her father cleared his throat. "Your mom and I were thinking maybe we'd sneak down to the cafeteria. Give you time to speak to the agents on your own. You feel up to doing that?"

Melinda could see her parents were struggling. Wanting

to know everything that had happened but being far too overwhelmed to take it all in at once.

She smiled. "Of course. Go have some breakfast." It would be easier this way. All the awful details. She needed the FBI to know so they could act.

Once they were alone, she began, "He played on my sympathetic side. That's how he got into my apartment. Said he was having a rough night…and needed a friend." Her stomach churned as she recalled just how trusting she'd been. "I can't believe I fell for his BS."

Special Agent Sullivan gave her a compassionate look. "Try not to be too hard on yourself. He knew exactly what he was doing and took advantage of your kindness. That's how criminals operate."

As Melinda went through the story of what had happened moment by moment, the agents listened intently and took notes. She recounted her fight with Corey and said it had ended with him shooting her, as she remembered only bits and pieces after that.

When the interview was over and they began to leave, Melinda's voice wavered as she asked two final questions. "What happens next? Will Corey stay in jail?"

Special Agent Russo closed her notebook and took a second to consider her answer. Her indigo eyes were filled with compassion and something else. Pride? "I can't promise anything, but we'll do everything we can to ensure he's prosecuted and convicted. Your statement today will be essential in that process."

Melinda watched them leave, feeling a mix of fear and hope over Corey's fate.

38

A month later, Lucas slid behind the wheel of the Ford as Journey *thunk*ed the passenger's side door closed.

She held up her phone. "Need me to punch Larson's address into the GPS?"

"No, thanks. It'll be burned into memory for a while." Or he figured it would. At least until the landmarks involved in another near tragedy replaced it. That was how his brain operated, reluctant to let go of events he wished he could change.

Journey pulled her notebook from her pocket, opened it to a blank page, and licked the tip of her pen like an old-timey reporter ready to take down the facts.

"Let me get this straight, Special Agent Sullivan. You have outstanding taste in coffee. You're generous in spirit, never overlooking a partner in need of caffeine or backup. On the asshole scale, rumor has it you rank embarrassingly low. I don't think Special Agent Russo had cause to call you an 'asshole' even once during this whole case."

"I—"

Journey held up a hand. "And if I might add...you and

your amazing partner prevented a pre-meditated murder, *plus* foiled a hostage situation in progress. Yet still you sound like the dog who caught the car. Tell us. What's the scoop?"

He smirked, then raised his middle finger from the wheel and let it stand there, speaking for him.

Journey laughed. "Now, what's an ace reporter done to deserve that?"

"Well, ace, you seem to have forgotten the four murders we didn't prevent. Plus, there's the missing thirteenth gun that hasn't turned up from Minton's street sales. Could be anywhere by now. What's your reporting say about them?"

Journey refused to break character. "The world's a cruel place, old chum. Keep your chin up and stay in the fight."

She was right, of course. He threw a quick smile her way. "Thanks, Journey."

"We did good work, Lucas." She lowered the notebook to her lap and squeezed his arm. "It's okay to hate that we couldn't do more. The striving keeps us hungry. I think the minute an agent starts thinking about their cases as lost causes, it's time to reconsider whether it's the cases that are the problem."

Not responding, Lucas pulled alongside the curb in front of Larson's place and parked. He spied Rob Larson himself staring out through the front window curtains as he and Journey came up the sidewalk.

On the stoop, before Lucas could lift his hand to knock, Larson opened the front door. "You said you had news."

Pauline Larson stood next to her ex-husband, her face expectant.

The agents had shared many long, quiet hours with the family at the hospital, each of their discussions focused on the *what-ifs*. Now they had actual news to share.

The kind Lucas preferred to deliver in person.

Inside, Melinda lay swaddled in blankets in her father's recliner, relaxing and almost healed from her injuries.

Lucas and Journey sat next to each other on the sofa, and he got down to business. "There was an avalanche of evidence against him. And once he realized that, Corey stopped acting as if he had reason to fight back. The confessions Journey overheard and recorded in Melinda's kitchen. The blood found on Norman Perry's shirt matched Minton's. The guns, the storage unit, Emmett Cohen's witness testimony and sketch. And, of course, your testimony, Melinda. He'll be serving mandatory life without parole."

Pauline Larson choked back tears. "I'm not usually a vengeful woman, but a part of me thinks a life sentence still isn't enough punishment."

Melinda lowered her gaze. "As long as he's locked away, that's good enough."

"Not for me, it's not." Rob Larson scoffed, his voice full of spite, but after a moment, he straightened his posture and changed his tone. "Forgive me. I'm the luckiest man alive. I need to remember that."

Journey waved away his embarrassment. "It's easy to forget the good things amid so much trauma."

Pauline moved to Larson's side and stroked his back. "I'll second that."

Lucas watched the loving exchange between Rob and Pauline with a tinge of jealousy. If he'd understood sooner the heavy toll his mother's murder would take on his life, maybe he and Serena would've been able to weather the storm that became their marriage. Hallie wouldn't have had to endure her parents' broken hearts or grow up dividing her time between households.

His career wouldn't have taken a ten-year detour in White-Collar Crimes.

But a person's future wasn't determined by *maybes* and *what-ifs*. The future depended on what you learned from your past. He saw that now, all these years later. Serena was happily remarried, and Hallie was growing into an amazing young woman. Anchorage was long gone, and he was moving forward. Lucas and his new partner had helped avert catastrophe.

On a recent phone call, Larson told Lucas that Melinda's assault had forced him to come clean with his wife about all the secrets he'd been keeping since Jerry Minton's death. They'd agreed to try to salvage their marriage one step at a time.

Lucas took in the three of them. Rob and Melinda had been given a second chance at life. Pauline had been granted the opportunity to help heal her family.

There was a tragedy. And then, there was hope.

He turned to Journey and gave her a small smile. "Anything to add?"

She smiled back. "No. I think it's time for us to move along and give these people their family time."

Give.

The word hit Lucas. Corey Minton had lost both parents and then taken more than that from those he judged responsible. But he hadn't completed his mission.

Together, they'd stopped him. Journey and Lucas, Melinda and her father, and everyone who'd touched the case in any small way had brought Corey's reign of terror to an abrupt end.

They had managed to give Rob, Melinda, and Pauline a chance at a future.

That was enough. At least for today.

39

Journey had nothing on her calendar for Saturday morning. She could've cleaned her apartment, gone grocery shopping, or paid her bills. A haircut would be necessary soon—her ends were splitting. And it was almost summer. Her heavier winter wardrobe would need a refresh.

But she didn't want to do any of those things. She wanted to spend time with her sister.

Michelle canceled the reservation she'd made at the yoga studio as soon as Journey called. "But we'll have to take Peanut for a walk. We both need the exercise."

Journey arrived with drinks, a chai tea latte for Michelle and her cup of black coffee, extra hot.

"What's the occasion?" Michelle pulled her front door closed and double-checked the dog's leash before accepting her cup. The day she adopted Peanut, she and Journey had gone to the rescue society together and come home with a white, ten-pound terrier mix with a brown circle of fur around his left eye. Journey claimed it looked like Mr. Peanut's monocle. Thus his name and the tradition of the doggie bow ties he wore daily.

Today's tie was baby blue with pink pinstripes. Journey had given it to him for Christmas. She pulled a treat from her pocket, holding it to Peanut's twitching nose before he gobbled it down. "The drinks are Lucas's influence. His good manners are rubbing off on me."

"Well, I like it." Michelle took a sip. "Ready to go?"

Her neighborhood was one of Pittsburgh's hidden gems, four or five quiet blocks of starter-family homes and duplexes. Noise came in the form of children's laughter. Police patrolled for opportunity theft, and there were open garage doors and deliveries left unattended on front porches rather than burglaries in progress.

It was just the oasis her sister needed and deserved after the trauma she'd endured.

"Congratulations on the Minton case." Michelle pointed to the left, and they headed down the block in the corresponding direction.

Journey *hmm*ed. "It's an amazing conclusion, considering how little evidence we found at the Faulkner and Perry scenes. A footprint, some stolen guns, and a few spots of blood that didn't belong to the victim."

That blood had proved a crucial link between Corey Minton and Norman Perry. Within hours of his arrest, they'd matched the types. DNA results later confirmed the blood was Corey's. Norman had gashed him with a knife during their struggle. Corey hadn't realized he'd left traces behind.

"We also had the shell casing you found in Lucklow's kitchen." Journey playfully elbowed her sister. "How could I manage to be the crack investigator I am without you?"

Michelle played along. "You wouldn't."

Journey laughed. "We're twinsies, you and I."

"Murder twins, more like. You gotta admit. We share some very strange interests."

"Oh, I don't know." Journey sipped her coffee. "Lots of

women are into fancy coffee drinks and murder and skateboarding these days."

Back in high school, Journey and Michelle had showed the boys they had what it took to join them in the park. Everything she'd learned during the days and months of struggling to master tricks had translated into Journey's tenacity in joining the FBI.

"Oh. That's it. We're the skateboarding Feds. Sounds like a TV show. We swoop in on our boards whenever trouble calls."

Journey stopped short. "Excuse me. Was that a joke I just heard come out of your mouth?"

"I'm in a good mood." Michelle winked and sipped her chai.

"I'll say."

"Hey, I'm proud of you. Your work on the Minton case was solid. You and Lucas saved the lives of his intended fifth and sixth victims."

Journey sighed. "I was trying to convince Lucas of the same thing the other day. That we need to take a win where we can get it. Easier to say it than believe it, I guess."

"Well, try to believe it. Or at least believe me." Michelle squeezed Journey's arm. "Because I'm pretty smart, you know. I graduated near the top of my class at Yale."

"You too?"

"Were you at Yale?" Michelle giggled. "I don't remember seeing you there."

"Two jokes in one morning?" Journey threw one hand into the air. "It's a miracle."

They walked on for a few minutes, enjoying the quiet, the sunshine, and their much-needed time together.

"Hey." Journey couldn't help but brag about one thing. "You didn't hear this from me, but one of the final nails in Corey's coffin was my statement under oath about what he admitted to at Melinda's town house. She was fading in and out of consciousness by then, so she could only repeat some of what she heard. But I knew the value of the words." Keeping track of details was her job as an FBI special agent, after all.

And to see a concrete connection between her work and the resolution of a case was the ultimate satisfaction.

Michelle smiled. "Look out, world. Agent Russo is on the case."

Journey mimed as if she were hopping onto her board. "Skating in to knock criminals off their feet."

Her phone vibrated in her pocket. Journey picked it up, finding her boss's name on the screen. "Hang on. It's Kenner." She moved to the edge of the sidewalk and answered. "Russo here."

"You and Sullivan need to get out to West Virginia. We've got a mass grave found in an abandoned mine."

The End

To be continued...

Thank you for reading.

All of *Journey Russo* series books can be found on Amazon.

ACKNOWLEDGMENTS

How does one adequately express gratitude to all those who have transformed a shared dream into a stunning reality? Let us attempt to do just that.

First and foremost, our families deserve our deepest thanks. Their unwavering support and encouragement have been our bedrock, allowing us the time and energy to translate our collective imagination into the words that fill these pages. Their belief in our vision has been a constant source of strength and inspiration.

As coauthors, our journey has been uniquely collaborative and rewarding. Now, with Mary also embracing the additional role of publisher, our adventure has taken on an exciting new dimension. This transition from solely writing to also publishing has been both a challenge and a joy, opening doors to share our work more directly with you, our readers.

We are immensely grateful to the entire team at Mary Stone Publishing — a group who believed in our potential from the very beginning. Their commitment extends beyond editing our words; it encompasses the tireless efforts of designers, marketers, and support staff, all dedicated to bringing our stories to life. Their expertise, creativity, and passion have been vital in capturing the essence of our tales and sharing them with the world.

However, our greatest appreciation is reserved for you, our beloved readers. You took a chance on our book, generously sharing your most precious asset—your time. It is our fervent hope that the pages of this book have rewarded that generosity, offering you a journey worth taking and memories that linger.

With all our love and heartfelt appreciation,

Mary & Amy

ABOUT THE AUTHOR

Mary Stone

Nestled in the serene Blue Ridge Mountains of East Tennessee, Mary Stone crafts her stories surrounded by the natural beauty that inspires her. What was once a home filled with the lively energy of her sons has now become a peaceful writer's retreat, shared with cherished pets and the vivid characters of her imagination.

As her sons grew and welcomed wonderful daughters-in-law into the family, Mary's life entered a quieter phase, rich with opportunities for deep creative focus. In this tranquil environment, she weaves tales of courage, resilience, and intrigue, each story a testament to her evolving journey as a writer.

From childhood fears of shadowy figures under the bed to a profound understanding of humanity's real-life villains, Mary's style has been shaped by the realization that the most complex antagonists often hide in plain sight. Her writing is characterized by strong, multifaceted heroines who defy traditional roles, standing as equals among their peers in a world of suspense and danger.

Mary's career has blossomed from being a solitary author to establishing her own publishing house—a significant milestone that marks her growth in the literary world. This expansion is not just a personal achievement but a reflection of her commitment to bring thrilling and thought-provoking stories to a wider audience. As an author and publisher, Mary continues to challenge the conventions of the thriller genre, inviting readers into gripping tales filled with serial killers, astute FBI agents, and intrepid heroines who confront peril with unflinching bravery.

Each new story from Mary's pen—or her publishing house—is a pledge to captivate, thrill, and inspire, continuing the legacy of the imaginative little girl who once found wonder and mystery in the shadows.

Discover more about Mary Stone on her website.
www.authormarystone.com

Amy Wilson

Having spent her adult life in the heart of Atlanta, her upbringing near the Great Lakes always seems to slip into her writing. After several years as a vet tech, she has dreams of going back to school to be a veterinarian but it seems another dream of hers has come true first. Writing a novel.

Animals and books have always been her favorite things, in addition to her husband, who wanted her to have it all. He's the reason she has time to write. Their two teenage boys fill the rest of her time and help her take care of the mini zoo that now fills their home with laughter…and yes, the occasional poop.

Connect with Mary online

facebook.com/authormarystone
x.com/MaryStoneAuthor
goodreads.com/AuthorMaryStone
bookbub.com/profile/3378576590
pinterest.com/MaryStoneAuthor
instagram.com/marystoneauthor
tiktok.com/@authormarystone